I0817860

Pseudologia Fantastica

First published in 2024 by Leilanie Stewart

ISBN: 9781739481933

The characters, events, names and places used in this book are fictitious or used fictitiously. Any resemblance to real persons, living or dead is coincidental.

Thank you for supporting independent publishing.

Website: www.leilaniestewart.com
F: facebook.com/leilaniestewartauthor
Twitter: @leilaniestewart
Instagram: @leilaniestewartauthor

Pseudologia Fantastica

Leilanie Stewart

Pseudologia Fantastica: Four stories of stalkers and mythomaniacs Envy. Lust. Control. Power. How far would a person go in their obsessive quest of another? In these two short stories and two novellas, ordinary people, going about their everyday lives, become the playthings of fantasists, who shape the narrative to achieve their ultimate goal: total domination over their targets. Will their innocent victims realise the dysfunctional game they are unwittingly a part of, before it is too late? £14.99

To Joe and KJ, who are always with me on the road less travelled.

Contents

Also by Leilanie Stewart

Belfast Ghosts Series

Book 1: The Blue Man
Book 2: The Fairy Lights
Book 3: Matthew's Twin

Other novels

The Buddha's Bone
Gods of Avalon Road

Short story Collections and Poetry

Diabolical Dreamscapes
The Redundancy of Tautology
A Model Archaeologist
Toebirds & Woodlice

One

Leah as the Artist's Muse

Leah stood at the bus stop, without an umbrella in the pouring rain. I saw her shivering and walked over. She looked up as I approached and blinked sending a shower of raindrops falling from her long eyelashes.

"You look freezing," I said.

"I am," she replied with a sniff, her nose red.

"Were you in church?" I said, jerking my head towards the Presbyterian Church across the road. Leah shook her head.

"Here, get under my umbrella until the bus comes," I said.

"No, I'm fine, seriously," she said, her teeth chattering.

Leah. Always too polite. I rolled my eyes, grinning.

"Do you really think I'm gonna stand here and let you die of hypothermia?" I said and she smiled. I held the umbrella over her head and a few minutes later, the number 35 bus came. Leah climbed on first.

"Thanks," she said, her summer dress clinging to her skin.

"No problem," I said, smiling. "You might not be a good Christian, but I am."

***

I spent the next day handing out flyers in the town centre. My church was planning a fete to raise money for a local hospice. The stalls of bric-a-brac usually drew in a few regulars who like bargain hunting, but the church wanted to draw in a younger crowd, so I volunteered to do some promotion.

As I talked about the fete to a couple of thirty-something women, Leah walked by. She didn't see me, busy browsing the clothes in shop windows.

"Hey, Leah!" I called.

She spun round. "Oh! George!"

"Wanna have one of these?"

Leah smirked. "More about church I see?"

"Why don't you come along some time? It's really not that bad," I said.

"No thanks, I'll pass," she said.

"Oh, come on," I teased. "We're having a fete and we could do with a few more young people around for the PR."

She shook her head. "It's not really my scene."

"Well, suit yourself," I said, smiling. "Doing some shopping?"

"Yeah," she said, tucking a strand of blonde hair behind her ear. "I should get going actually. I'm meeting a friend."

I nodded. "I'm glad to see you're dressed in better clothes in case we get another shower."

Leah fished a pocket-umbrella out of her bag. "I'm prepared this time."

"Alright then, catch you later," I said. Leah grinned and sauntered away down the street.

***

"So why don't you ask her out?" said my friend, Stevie.

"Ask who out?"

"This girl you keep going on about. Leah."

"Oh – her." I shook my head. "No."

"Why not? Sounds your type. Young, blonde. And the way you went on about her summer dress clinging to her."

I screwed up my face. "It's not like that, she's a friend. I felt sorry for her, she was drenched. If you'd seen her in that dress, she was so pathetic."

"Yeah, that's what you say," said Stevie, raising his eyebrows.

"Believe what you want," I said. "I'm a man of church, I don't take advantage of people. But still..."

"Yeah, I knew it. Admit it–"

"There's something about her. Something I can't work out."

"Bad?"

I shook my head. "This fragility about her. I just don't know her that well and she keeps her distance."

"Sounds like she's toying with you," said Stevie. "Playing hard to get. I tell you, she wants you to come and get her."

***

After work, I took a shortcut through the university campus on my way to the bus-stop. The green lawn smelled fresh after the past few days' rain. I inhaled, enjoying life as I weaved among the students leaving their last classes of the day.

As I walked by the university cafeteria, I glanced in and saw Leah sitting with a friend. She was busy talking over soup and a bread roll. The café was open for another half hour, and as the last couple of stragglers left, I ducked in to say hello.

"Leah," I said and pulled up a chair.

"George," she said with a surprised smile.

"Who's this?" I said, looking at the brunette with her.

"Heather, this is George. George, Heather."

I shook hands with Heather.

"Are they still serving?" I asked. "Might as well get dinner while I'm here."

"No, café's nearly closing. Actually, we'd better be off," said Leah.

"There's no rush," said Heather, flicking her hair off her shoulder. "I wouldn't mind grabbing a drink."

"You're old enough to drink?' I joked, 'Drinking's bad for you."

Leah squeezed her friend's hand. "He's Christian, he doesn't drink."

"Oh, you're Christian?" said Heather. "What church do you go to? I used to go to St Mark's near–"

I heard a thump as the table rattled. Leah looked red. "Ow!" she said. "I banged my knee."

"Well, that'll stop you from running off then," I teased.

"No really, we'd better go," said Leah, dropping the rest of her bread roll in her soup. "We have a lot of research to do, right Heather?"

"What do you study?" I asked.

"Media studies," said Heather, with a flirtatious grin. I looked at Leah. She looked tired, probably with all the coursework.

"Well, good luck with all the research," I said. Leah smiled and gave me a wave as they left.

***

My car was finally fixed: my beat-up little old Ford Fiesta. The insurance covered the damage, but the accident bumped my premium another £300 to £1500 a year. I didn't care that much. It was nice not to have to take the bus.

Lunchtime traffic was bad. I felt as though I'd been stuck at the zebra crossing for hours as streams of students passed by. One of the faces caught my eye. Like Leah, but maybe a few years younger.

I rolled down my window. "Hello there," I said.

The girl turned. Definitely like Leah, only she had to be sixteen, or seventeen.

"Do you have a sister called Leah?" I asked.

"Yeah," she said smiling, "Do I know you?"

"No. I'm a friend of your sister's."

She walked over. "Oh, you must be George. She talks about you."

"Where are you off to?" I asked, noting her green blazer and skirt. "Shouldn't you be in school?"

"Lunch break," she said, in a sing-song voice. "Technically I'm not meant to as only sixth-formers are allowed off school grounds, but hey, I'm nearly sixteen."

I tutted in a teasing way. "I won't tell your sister."

"Thanks. She didn't tell me how nice you are."

"What's your name anyway?"

"Liberty," she said. "Well goodbye."

"Bye now."

***

I parked in a narrow back street close to the shopping mall. I had just enough time on my lunch break to pick up a present for my mother's eightieth birthday. Her birthday fell on the Sunday of that week, so I planned to give it to her after church.

In front of the shopping mall's huge glass doors, three promotion girls wearing hot-pants and caps, gave out flyers for a mobile phone offer. I shook my head at the scantily-clad women, irritated by the distraction, until one of them caught my eye. Leah.

She looked different to how she usually appeared with make-up heavy on her face. Her demeanour seemed more extroverted too, which didn't suit her. Her legs were thinner than I had imagined, and she seemed fragile underneath the facade, like a china-doll.

"Hi. Do you know you have a phone sticking out of your head?" I joked.

Leah's kohl-lined eyes were wide with surprise. "Oh yeah, this?" she said, tapping the plastic phone attached to her cap. "Part of the job. Fancy meeting you here anyway George."

"Gotta get a gift for my mum. What about you? Do you work for this phone company?"

"No, a modelling agency. Most of the jobs are fun, but sometimes I have to wear silly stuff like this."

I looked down at the hot-pants. "Well, not sure it suits you entirely."

Leah managed an awkward grin. "It pays the university fees, that's all that matters."

"I'll take a leaflet for your trouble. Maybe you can take one for my church fete in exchange," I said, grinning, and walked into the shopping mall.

***

I slowed my car down as I approached the green-clad girls. The one in the middle of the trio was definitely Liberty, and it definitely looked like there was going to be rain.

I tooted my horn and wound down the window. "Hi Liberty."

"Er – George, isn't it?"

"That's right. I saw your sister yesterday out doing her stuff on the town."

"Yeah, she said she saw you."

"Wanna lift home? I can drop all you girls off."

Liberty and her girl-friends leaned their heads close together. "...He's religious. Guess it's a Christian thing to do..."

"No thanks," said one of Liberty's friends. "We'll walk."

"Where do you live? Near here?" I asked.

The girls linked arms and stood staring at me, chewing their gum.

"Kind of. Not far. We can walk," said Liberty. "But thanks."

The rain drummed against the windows. A fleeting thought of those poor girls crossed my mind as I emptied my groceries onto the kitchen counter. None of them had their blazers, nor seemed to be carrying jackets, or umbrellas of any kind. I pictured them running, soaked to the skin, their uniforms clinging to them, and their hair matted. I wondered if I should have gone back to pick them up, but I let the thought go. I had to call my mum to check if her electricity was holding up alright through the storm. On a night like this, she would be frightened in her house alone. Noise, even loud rain made her think burglars might take advantage of the distraction and come.

I dialled the number and waited. There was no answer. I hung up.

Strange. Mum usually sat close to the phone. I tried again, punching in the familiar keys.

A young woman's voice answered. "Hello?"

Who could that be? Did my mum have a home-help? "Hello?" said the young woman, impatience clear in her tone.

I hung up a second time. A housekeeper: that had to be it. I dialled again.

"Hello? Who is this? If this is someone playing a joke, it's not funny," said the young woman, sounding breathless.

I put the receiver down, my heart thudding in my chest. Was Mum okay? Once again, I dialled.

"Who *is* this?" said the young woman, her voice panicked. "I'm calling the police, this isn't funny."

I slammed the receiver down, making a gust of wind blow the leaflets from my printer next to the phone onto the floor. I picked up the print-outs and shuffled them into a pile, ready to hand out tomorrow. That would get my mind off my worries: my mum, the girls in the rain, and fearful voice of the young woman on the phone.

***

I ran my finger along the spines of the books. The university bookstore had the best Christian-science section in town, and for the best prices. I pulled a thin volume off a shelf and leafed through it. The illustrations were pleasant to look at and reminded me of the oil-paintings that I had dabbled in during my youth. I often thought that I would like to get back into art.

From the corner of my eye, a flash of long, golden hair caught my eye. I turned and saw Leah browsing the titles in the classical studies section nearby. Her chin jutted upwards giving her long neck a graceful line as she looked at the books on the highest shelf. Her cream-coloured skirt had a thigh-high split and I couldn't help but admire the gentle asymmetrical outline that her legs made against the linear books. From the crest of her calf upwards past the rounded rump of her bottom to the trough of her back and onwards to the right angle of her shoulder blade near her neck,

I couldn't help but see before me an artist's dream, a faint halo around her from the backdrop of afternoon sun.

I slid up beside her. "Small world. We keep bumping into each other."

She turned her head, wrecking the perfect pose. "Oh, hi. Yes, quite the coincidence. So, eh – are you buying books?"

"More church studies," I said. "They have the most elegant artwork, churches."

Leah tucked her hair behind her ear, looking down at the open book in my hand.

"I used to do some painting. I've been meaning to get back into it," I said.

"That's nice," said Leah, a faint smile curling the corners of her mouth.

"Yes, I think life painting is best. The way they paint the Madonna and child. I don't know how they mix the paint so white for their skin," I said.

"It's amazing, isn't it?" she said.

"You have such nice skin. Has anyone ever painted you?" I asked.

"Oh no, not me," said Leah, a blush coming to her cheeks. She shook her head, dislodging the blonde strand that was tucked behind her ear.

"You have a statuesque grace even though you're so petite. I'd be interested in painting you sometime, if you'd like–"

Leah pressed her lips into a tight smile. "That's okay. I'm not interested," she said.

"Well, the offer's there if you change your mind. It would be like your other modelling jobs only it would take a bit longer. You could bring your sister along too; I think she'd look good on canvas as well."

"Liberty has too much work at the minute with her GCSEs," said Leah, taking a few steps backwards. "And I'm quite busy with my coursework too to be honest, George."

She turned away from me. I watched her leave the shop, hugging her folder close to her chest. With her head hanging and her stooped walk, she no longer had the poise of a deity.

***

The drive to the superstore took forty minutes. The main road leading into Birchfield was choc-a-block at rush hour. Still, it was worth the wait. The superstore had the best selection of birthday cakes and I wanted to get a good one for mum.

I got myself a trolley and walked in through the crowded entrance. A small, middle-aged woman with blonde hair, about my age struggled out laden with bags.

"Are you okay there?" I asked her.

She stopped puffing and looked up. "I'm getting my exercise for the year," she said with a smile.

"Can I give you a hand at all?"

"Thank you, that's very kind," she said.

I took half of her load out of her burdened hands. "Do you live far?" I asked.

"About a ten-minute walk," she said.

I looked out at the main road, still heavy with traffic. Either a ten-minute walk or a twenty-minute wait in a heated car; it was the coldest summer on record.

"My car's parked over there," I said pointing.

"Why, that's very kind of you," she said.

"We have a motto at Greyvale Church to do at least one good deed a day."

"Greyvale? But that's on the other side of the town," said the woman. "I hope I'm not making you go out of your way too much?"

I shook my head. "It's no bother to me, no trouble at all."

***

Briar Court was a quiet cul-de-sac. After I helped the woman with her shopping, I turned my car at the end of the street. She waved from the doorstep of the brown-brick semi-detached house, and I tooted and waved back. Before I pulled out of the street, three green-clad girls rounded the corner. I saw the blonde-girl in the middle gape as she looked at my car and then the nearest one, a thin, black-haired creature banged the hood of my little Fiesta. Hooligans.

***

Toothbrush. Toothpaste. Shaving cream. Check. I placed the items in my basket and made my way to the counter. Ahead of me in the queue was a familiar head of long, blonde hair.

I leaned close. “Hello,” I whispered.

Leah jumped. “George!” she said, her eyes watery. She looked down at my basket. “You shop here?”

I shrugged. “I was in the area, so I thought I’d pick up a few things. What are you getting?”

I saw the package in her hands: tampons. She fumbled as she tried to hide it, but not quickly enough.

“Why are you doing this?” she asked.

“Doing what? Asking about what you’re getting? I know it’s tampons, but you shouldn’t be ashamed about your time of the month. Friends don’t care about those things.”

“We aren’t friends,” said Leah. She hurried out of the shop, dropping the tampons on the aisle floor.

I watched her rush into the crowded mall. I set down my basket and tried to follow, but she had gone. Then, from somewhere among the stream of shoppers, I heard her voice.

“There he is. That’s him with the grey moustache.”

I felt a strong hand on my shoulder. “Excuse me mate,” said a deep male voice.

I turned around. A security guard glowered at me. Leah stood in front of a shop with another security guard. She wiped her mascara-stained cheeks. Her face looked blotchy.

“What’s going on?” I asked. The security guard led me over to Leah and stood on her other side. She was tiny in the middle of the two men, cradling her arms.

"He's been following me for weeks. He won't leave me alone," said Leah, hiccoughing.

"Following you?" I said, feeling heat rise in my face. "You've got me wrong. We're friends."

"He followed me onto the bus one evening. He wasn't even getting the 35, he got on just to corner me to find out stuff. It was all just a ploy to talk to me. He even got off at the next stop! He has a car, he doesn't need to take the bus," Leah babbled.

I looked at each of their faces in turn, shocked at Leah's words. "You don't believe this, do you? I'm a Christian! I was being a good friend – she was soaked when I met her!"

"Oh yeah?" said Leah, sniffing back tears. "Coming into the student canteen at my university when it's not for the public? I had to kick my friend Heather under the table because she was giving away too much information about herself, and pretend I banged my knee!"

"You harassed this girl at her university?" said one of the security men. "I know Leah – she did modelling promotions with my wife. She wouldn't lie."

"He found out who my sister was and even tried to get her to come into his car. She's only fifteen!" Leah gasped.

"I only wanted to give her a lift home since you and I are friends."

"We aren't friends! I don't even know you. Why would I be friends with a man old enough to be my dad? I'm only nineteen."

"If Leah says she doesn't know you, then why would you want to be friends?" asked the other security man.

"I don't know – she's upset," I said.

"He even tricked my mum into getting into his car and drove her home, so now he knows where I live," she said, wiping fluid from her nose. I wrinkled my face in disgust. Leah looked better when she was immaculate, not a red-faced blubbering liar.

"And what's more – I've been getting crank calls," said Leah. "All I can hear is a man breathing down the phone when I answer. I dialled one four seven one and got a number from the Greyvale area, and that's where he lives. I'm pretty sure it's him."

"Is this true?" asked one of the security men. "Have you been calling her up too?"

I shrugged. "I've dialled a few wrong numbers by mistake once or twice. It only takes one wrong key when I'm calling my mum and I ring someone else."

"It's on purpose." Leah sobbed, her voice shaking. "He followed me here today – he wasn't even shopping. Look – he's got nothing."

The security men were tight-lipped. "We could easily review the CCTV footage and have you arrested. Do you realise this, mate?"

"Arrested?" I said, clenching my fists. "I haven't even touched this girl!"

"But you would have if you got the chance!" Leah's shouting caused a few shoppers to stare. "He even asked me to pose for him so he could paint me. What he meant was naked!"

"I never said that!" I yelled back.

"You implied it," she screamed. "You said I had nice skin and talked about statuesque grace or something creepy like that!"

"You live in Greyvale?" asked one of the guards.

I nodded.

"Then what business brings you to Birchfield?"

"Nothing. I like it here."

"He doesn't even work – and he's not Christian either. Greyvale Church hasn't even heard of a George. I rang them," said Leah, tears streaking down her face.

The security men looked serious. "Do you know what you've done? You don't have to touch someone to harass them. This is called psychological abuse. You're stalking this girl. There are anti-harassment laws in this country, didn't you know?"

I gritted my teeth, letting the words sink in. "Okay, fine. I don't have a job, so what? I spend my time looking for new friends. That's my business. And maybe I don't go to church, but the sentiment is there – I'm a good Christian who helps other people and befriends the needy. And this is how I get repaid? I don't stalk this girl – but I know everything about her if I wanted to: where she works, lives, goes to university, and goes out with friends. And I think the world has come to be an ugly place, if this is what happens to charitable people. What would God think of how you've treated me? I can rest easy in that knowledge."

Two

Dog Days of Doom

NICKY

"I'd like to give a warm welcome to Adenike Odelola, author of *Dog Days of Doom*, the stunning psychological thriller that is set in our wonderful city. Am I saying that right, Aid-Nike?"

"Adda-knee-kay." I said phonetically, with a reassuring smile; I didn't want to make my host, Sam, feel awkward because of their mispronunciation. "Most folks know me as Nicky, so please call me that."

"Nicky, of course." Sam smiled at me before turning to the camera, live-streaming the event. "We're happy to have Nicky here tonight as our first Author Spotlight at *Bookish Buns*. Usually, we have a few open mic poetry slots, but we've never had a fiction writer come along, so we're very excited to talk about your debut novel, which has taken our city by storm."

Sam's red face and fluster showed their embarrassment at mispronouncing my name; not only in front of the audience in their own café but to possibly hundreds of followers tuning in on *Bookish Buns*' live stream, no less. It really didn't bother me; Nicky was a much catchier moniker that everyone, even my own family, called me ever since I was a child.

Personally, I always made sure to get people's names, and pronouns, correct. It was only polite and showed due consideration of others. Sam, the owner of *Bookish Buns*, with their short purple hair and thick black glasses, made it clear on their website that they were a 'they and them' and I respected that. Diversity, in my opinion, was a blessing on any city, and multiculturalism enhanced the artistic flavour of a locality. This city had certainly improved in the past decade, since migrants had entered and added their expertise to the inner-city neighbourhoods.

Sam jolted me from my musings.

"So, Nicky, could we start with maybe a short summary of your book, *Dog Days of Doom* for the audience tonight who may not have read your book yet? I for one loved it and can't imagine anyone who hasn't read it yet – but you never know!"

I smiled again, then cleared my throat. "Well, as the title suggests, it's set in the middle of summer, in this very city. Strange occurrences have been happening – threatening notes sent to some small business owners signed by 'The Black Dog' as well as property damage – and sightings of a mysterious dark-hooded figure, but even the police seem to have lost any leads of what is happening. When two business owners get together to seek vigilante justice, the Black Dog turns his attention to them on a sinister crusade that involves one being framed for murder and the other almost being burned alive in an arson attack. Can the plucky pair find out the identity of The Black Dog and save the city from certain doom?"

"Thanks for sharing that synopsis with our audience. Wow, what can I say? Even though I binge read *Dog Days of Doom* in two nights, no less, hearing that summary all over again gets me fired up to re-read it again. What was your inspiration for the character of The Black Dog?"

I took a deep breath, gathering my thoughts. "To be honest, Sam, I drew inspiration from fear itself. I think when people are beset by problems, it's human nature to want to attribute blame to a mysterious source. Only, in the case of my story, I decided to manifest that fear into an actual person – an underworld criminal – who was targeting small business owners, particularly those of ethnic minority backgrounds – and trying to drive them out."

Sam narrowed their eyes in a pensive affectation. "So, was racism a motivation for your book?"

I cocked my head. "Not per se. It wasn't a driving factor for the story. As you'll know since you've read it, the gay bakery owner gets threatened, as does the elderly greengrocer who owns her shop on valuable land close to the city centre. The Black Dog has various motivations, it isn't as cut-and-dry as racism alone. It's a complex story – or at least, I hope it comes across that way."

Sam smiled, their eyes crinkling to slits. "I loved the use of local vernacular in the book. I really think it made the story more authentic and stand out more from some other crime thrillers that are quite well known. Did you have to do much research in terms of the colloquial parts of the book?"

I paused. Was my host serious? "Well, as you *might* know, I'm from here. My mum is a local. My dad, who was Nigerian, died a few years ago but they both raised me here. So, I'm well acquainted with the slang."

"Of course." Another blush formed on Sam's cheeks. "I think we'll take a few questions now, if anyone has any?"

I looked at the rows of chairs, filling the café. *Bookish Buns* was open by day as a literary café where customers could buy a Sylvia Plath bun or an Edgar Allan Poe cake, and borrow books to read from shelves that lined the walls. For the evening Author Spotlight event, the round tables had been pushed aside and the wooden chairs arranged in five rows of ten. All fifty seats had been filled, with more people standing at the back.

One woman towards the middle put up her hand and I gestured to her my acknowledgement.

"Would you say you're happy with how your book has been received?" she asked.

"Yes, I'm pleased that readers find the main characters likeable and find their fears relatable, especially in how they handled the Black Dog figure. I'm very happy that people seem to like my story, especially since it's my first book. It's what every author wants to hear. The feedback has been very supportive and encouraging," I said.

My eyes travelled away from her towards another woman sitting in the front row towards the far right side. She looked to be in her mid-forties and had frizzy dark hair with a heavy fringe. Her pink plastic glasses, denim pinafore with cartoon cherub designs and *Ugg* boots gave her the appearance of someone eager to appear younger than their years; or at least, younger at heart. A heavy-set woman of mid-thirties appearance with straggly blonde hair leaned close and whispered in the dark-haired woman's ear. The blonde woman wore a long, black, bohemian style skirt and I noted a pentagram hanging on a chain around her neck, which dangled among the folds of a knitted jumper. Both women giggled in a way more reminiscent of adolescents than fully mature women, before composing themselves. I let my eyes scan the room in search of another question; there would always be people opposed to my work. I was used to that as an author; though it did make me wonder, what had I said that was so funny?

Sam seemed to have read my mind, for they pointed at the blonde woman. "Lisa, what do you think about the notion of small business owners being under threat by a mysterious criminal figure? Have you ever heard of this sort of thing happening that you can think of?"

Lisa puckered her face and sniffed. "In the town I grew up in, there was a criminal gang who came in and were running drugs in the place – nobody ever saw them, as they used kids to do the actual dealing in schools and so on, but there was this one abandoned old mansion near the train station, and you would sometimes see lights on during the evening, even though it had been derelict for so long–"

As Lisa droned on, I couldn't help but notice how charismatic she was, and how she certainly loved the sound of her own voice. Once she had monopolised the attention of the whole room, she added in a few quips that amused a smattering of people, gesticulating widely for effect. I found myself zoning out and waited until she had finished relaying her anecdote about the criminals in the town where she had spent her teenage years getting their comeuppance.

"Nicky, getting back to your story, do you have a sequel planned for *Dog Days of Doom*, or is it going to be a one-off novel?"

"It's a good question," I started. "I had intended it as a standalone novel, but honestly, I wasn't expecting it to do so well and on the basis of that, I might outline a sequel – or who knows, even a trilogy."

Sam slapped their hands against their legs in excitement. "Oh, you can bet that I for one will be following your Socials closely for updates about any more books in the series."

I reached for a sip of my now lukewarm tea that Sam had provided before the live stream started and took a bite of the delicious vegan brownie that they had baked specially. Once I had dabbed crumbs from my lips, I thanked my host and the audience for having me along to do an author Q and A. It had been a successful night.

***

"Goodnight Nevaeh, baby, Mummy's home. I love you."

My seven-year-old daughter blew a long puff of air in response, deep in her dream.

I turned to smile at my husband, Neil, standing in her open bedroom doorway. He grinned back.

"Thanks for getting her to go down so early. I was worried she'd still be up, demanding to watch *Gabby's Dollhouse,* or something."

"She was alright. I gave her milk and a cookie, and she loved the new plush unicorn you got her, worked a treat." Neil jerked his thumb towards Nevaeh's bed. "She's got it under the covers with her."

Nevaeh had been a bit clingy over the past couple of months. My book success had taken me further afield while doing book signings and literary festivals, and she was used to me being there for her evening and bedtime routine. Neil's cooking was competent, but basic for Nevaeh who was used to my fancier culinary dishes; they had taken to ordering pizza on occasion when she had refused his dinners while I had been away. On takeaway nights, Nevaeh would end up bouncing off the walls, probably at all the additives in whatever feast they had ordered. I was glad the plush unicorn had at least helped to settled her; I had cuddled with it for the whole day beforehand while Nevaeh had been at school, to make sure my scent was on it. It was a trick I had learned about how to get babies to settle when going to day care; apparently it worked on an older child too.

Neil kissed me, after closing Nevaeh's bedroom door behind me. "How was the event?"

"You know, I think it went well. Everyone there seemed to like the book pretty much." I wrinkled my nose. "Well, most people anyway. There were one or two in the audience who seemed non-plussed, but everyone was polite and respectful I'd say."

"Sounds like a huge success. So, what shall we watch on the box to celebrate?"

***

MICHELLE

Dog Days of Doom. What a stupid, flippin' title, if ever I'd heard one. What was the big deal about that woman's book? Not like there weren't a million local authors with much better books than hers.

My Yorkie, Jaffa, raced out into the hall to greet me, making sure the evening wasn't a complete waste of time.

"Aww, how's my wittle Jaffa-waffa? Have you been a good girl while Mummy was away?"

Jaffa dashed away into the living room, her tail wagging. I followed with a grin. My girls always gave the pick-up I needed.

I plonked myself on the plush sofa and winced. As I lifted my left butt cheek, I slid my crochet needles out from where I had left them. Biscuit's half-finished doggy coat slid off the needle.

"Oh, fiddlesticks!"

As I fed my crochet work back onto the needle, I waited for the laptop to boot up. My fundraiser page popped up on the screen: *Save dogs from dinner plates.*

One hundred pounds.

My heart swelled. One hundred pounds was a great start in saving those poor dogs from a terrible fate in cramped Chinese cages were they would end up on some awful person's dinner plate. It would take at least two thousand pounds to be able to get them to the border of Korea, and from there, we could staff enough people to smuggle them out with the necessary paperwork to get them onto ships headed for the UK.

It made me shudder to think of all of those dogs, with their sad eyes peering out of cages, waiting for a kind human being to help them. I smiled to myself. That person was me. I was one of the best human beings there was. Most people liked to give a pound here or there to charity, mostly so they could feel better about themselves for doing a good deed rather than actually making a change to someone's life. But not me. I was proactive. I had set up the fundraiser and was actively getting donations to help rescue dogs from dinner plates.

Jaffa jumped up beside me, wagging her tail. I grabbed her into a big cuddle and smothered her with kisses. My Yorkie was one of those dogs I had saved. How many others would safely reach our shores?

My lovely wife walked through from the kitchen, distracting me from my musings. She was carrying a plate of chocolate digestives. Her black bob was tucked behind her ears allowing the blonde curtains at the front to fall forward; very sexy.

"Mmm, you got my favourite. You're so sweet. How is it you can read my mind?" I said.

She bent to kiss me, before plopping down on the sofa and sending Jaffa diving for safety on the armrest. "I know you so well, that's all. You're an open book."

"Well, I do wear my heart on my sleeve," I gushed, my chest swelling at all the praise and attention.

"How was the event, Snowbie?"

My wife had taken to calling me by the nickname because of my penchant for cute Snow Angel designs on pretty much everything: my favourite pinafore dress, my cooking apron, my handbag, my short story notebook; the list was endless. That and, ahem, my generous waistline these days, which made me kind of look like an overgrown cherub. I loved the nickname. It gave the impression of something cute, and cuddly; just like me.

I closed my laptop with a click. "It was alright. It would've been better if it was the usual open mic format though. I didn't much like that awful woman that Sam invited."

"Oh yeah, that crime writer? Rather gorgeous Nubian woman."

I blanched. "Gorgeous? What? And she's Nigerian, by the way, not Nubian. Though with the way she wears those dangling braids on her fringe and around her face, you'd think she fancies herself as an ancient Egyptian. She's no Cleopatra. As if she could be that beautiful. Ugh."

Ash puckered her face. "I thought you loved braids. You did when I got them done last year for the Sisters of the Solstice festival."

"Yeah, well they looked good on you, but not *her.*"

"What's got your knickers in a twist then? Was Adenike rude to you or something?"

"It's *Nicky*, please, not *Ada*-Nicky." I feigned a theatrical voice. "Can you imagine the demands of that woman, correcting Sam and embarrassing them in front of their own café? Such a rude *bitch*."

"You don't like *her*, then, not the book?" Ash cocked her head, in a cute, playful manner that I loved when she was enquiring something of me.

"I don't like her *or* her book. Have you tried to read it? It's horrible. So grim and depressing, it gives a bad impression of this city. You'd think if anyone abroad was reading it, they'd think it's all crime and locals hating on foreigners here, nothing good going for it." I grabbed my crochet needles and started feeding them through the unfinished doggy coat.

Ash sighed. "Well, I haven't read the book, so I can't say if it was good or not. Crime and thrillers aren't my thing anyway. Gimme vampire romance any day."

"At least it was a one-off event. No chance of me seeing that woman again, if I can help it." I sniffed.

"Unless she becomes a regular. What if she starts coming to the open mic nights?"

I glared at Ash. "Oh, that would be the worst! I'd have to have a quiet word with Sam if she did that. Though thankfully, she isn't a poet. At least, I don't think she is."

My gaze drifted to the side of the room where my Snow Angel notebook lay on the TV stand. I wasn't much good at poetry myself, but I had tried to write a few poems, mainly to fit in at the open mic nights. The first time I had read one of my poems, my hands had shaken so much, I had needed to stop in the middle as I couldn't keep the book still enough to read the words. Short stories were more my thing. I had a flair for writing the short form, even if I said so myself.

"Well, she certainly wouldn't need to be a poet – her book is doing well it seems," Ash droned on. "Didn't *Dog Days of Doom* reach the top ten for new crime-book releases, or something?"

I puckered my lips on purpose, making Ash laugh at my duck-lips. "Ugh, don't you think that title is just the worst?"

Ash guffawed a bit more at my silly expression, then composed herself. "It's certainly catchy, I'll give her that."

"Hey, whose side are you on? You're meant to back me up, here!" I grabbed a Snow Angel cushion and batted Ash with it.

"Come on now, Michelle. You aren't jealous of her – are you?"

I blanched. "What do you take me for? What would I have to be jealous of? I'll prove it to you."

I set my crocheting down and strode across to grab my writing book.

"Ooh, am I actually going to get to read this mystery story you've been working on, then?" Ash rubbed her palms together and reached for the book.

I whisked it to my left and gave her a teasing smile. "Nah, uh uh! Not so quick, missus quick-fingers. You get to listen."

I cleared my throat and stood in the centre of the room, as though I was reading in front of an audience at *Bookish Buns*.

"It was a rainy and thunderous night. The overcast sky covered the landscape and looked down on the town with an angry grey scowl. The man carefully stepped outside the shack, making sure to put up his umbrella quickly because the raindrops pelted down like missiles–"

Ash's cackling broke my flow and I stopped reading. She rolled her head back and clapped her hands, stamping her fluffy slippers on the carpet.

"What's so funny? You shouldn't be laughing. It's a gothic horror, not a comedy," I said, folding my arms.

"Listen, Snowbie, you know I'm your biggest fan. I loved some of the poems you read at *Bookish Buns* – and didn't I clap the loudest of anyone there?"

"Ye-ss," I said, lowering my eyes. What was Ash getting at? "But?"

Ash took a deep breath. "But your opening there could do with some work."

I snapped my notebook shut and folded my arms. "Such as?"

My wife put her hands up in a gesture of appeasement. "Look, maybe now isn't the right time. Why don't we watch some TV and talk about the fundraiser instead?"

I hardened my jaw. "No, I need to hear this. What's so wrong with my opening that you find so funny?"

"Well." Ash tucked a strand of her black bob behind her ear. "It's just that you've done the classic writing no-no of opening with *It was a dark and stormy night* for a start. Then the bit about the sky having an 'angry grey scowl' is kind of amateurish. It reeks of novice writer."

"It's called pathetic fallacy, for your information," I snapped.

"No, sweetie, pathetic fallacy is, if the rain in your story reflected the man's mood. The weather having human feelings is personification, Snowbie. Then you've got an adverb next – carefully – followed by another adverb – quickly – which is another creative writing no-no. You should use adverbs sparingly, only if they're absolutely necessary. After that, you describe the rain as pelting down like missiles. Well, it's a bit hyperbolic, that's all."

"It's not hyperbolic, it's using similes. Similes are good, don't tell me they're a writing no-no too, cause they aren't!"

She sighed. "Similes are fine. But you should save hyperbole for an action scene; it would have more effect, trust me. If you used subtlety in your opening scene, it would create a much more sinister, and ominous set-up for your story."

I knew it was immature, but I couldn't help myself; I stamped my left foot down so hard that Jaffa leapt off the sofa in fright and I flung my notebook across the room with such a clatter, it knocked my *Game of Thrones* 'pop figure' *Danerys* off the TV stand. Thank goodness Jaffa hadn't gone for it; her teeth digging in would've made me regret it later.

"Sinister? Ominous? Fancy words, missus fancy-pants! Alright, teacher! If you're so smart, why don't *you* write a story then, hmm?"

Ash's hands went up again and I could imagine she would have waved a white peace flag, if she'd had one. "I didn't mean to schoolmarm you there. Look, really, I didn't mean to cause offense. I think your story has great potential – that's why I'm giving you feedback in the first place."

"Feedback? It's abuse," I cried, a tear springing to the corner of my eye.

"It's constructive criticism, honey. I give comments like this to my GCSE and A-level students all the time, and you know what? They take it. They make changes to their stories for the better."

"Oh, so now I'm more immature than a stupid teenager?" I huffed, turning my back on her.

Ash shook her head. "I wasn't saying that at all. Listen, Michelle, I'm sorry. Can we forget this? I'm sorry I laughed. And I'm sorry I offended you. Please don't give up on your dreams. I want to hear the rest of that story. Is it finished?"

I wiped my tears away and turned back round to face her. "Not yet. I have writer's block. I don't really know what the horror in the story is, just that the man was in the shack because he's keeping something secret, and when he unleashes it, it's going to turn everyone in the town into zombies."

"Great." Ash's eyes were wide and hopeful. "Well, that sounds like a good premise that you can build off. Keep writing it and when it's done, I'll be in the front row of *Bookish Buns*, ready to cheer you on when you read it."

***

NICKY

One.

One star.

A one-star rating. But no review.

I'd had all four and five star reviews so far, not even a three star review, and now this.

My eyes hurt looking at the bright screen in the dark room, but I didn't want to wake Neil and Nevaeh up by switching on the living room light. My insomnia was sadly for a good reason; I stared at the bad rating in disbelief. I had to be rational; that was the nature of writing. If you put your work out there you invited criticism as much as praise. Nobody was universally popular.

Then again, there was a difference between criticism and a hater. I studied the thumbnail profile photo, leaning closer to my computer to see the image. The headshot showed a woman with shoulder-length dark hair, a blunt fringe and red framed spectacles. Her chin was inclined at a tilt to the right, giving her a mischievous look. Although she was at least a decade younger in the photo, ten pounds slimmer and the image had been heavily brightened with filters applied, there was no mistaking it; it was the forty-something brunette from *Bookish Buns* who had been wearing the cherub covered pinafore dress and pink glasses. The profile name said 'Michelle Connor'.

I thought back to that event, a week before. Michelle had given me no indication on that evening that she hated my book so much. Apart from giggling when her blonde-haired friend had whispered a no-doubt derogatory opinion at my expense, she had been a benign and attentive listener in the audience. She had neither asked questions, nor pulled any faces, presenting a totally neutral demeanour.

There was only one option; I had to enquire about why she would wait a week, and then post a one-star rating. Sam would be the best person to contact, since it was their event. My mind was made up; I would send a quick, friendly email to Sam, asking if there had been any feedback after the event from anyone in the audience.

***

MICHELLE

"She asked what?"

I was sure that if my mobile phone had feelings, it would've been screaming in agony at my fingernails digging into it; I held it away from my ear and looked at Sam's name on the screen.

"She said you had left a one-star rating of Dog Days of Doom and she wanted to know if you had said anything about it after she left Bookish Buns, as she felt it was very random," said Sam.

Harumph to that horrible cow, Nicky. "How did she know it was me? I never introduced myself that night."

"I don't know, Michelle." Sam paused. I could sense her thinking on the other end of the phone. "Could she have recognised your profile photo?"

I huffed, sending my fringe flying upwards in a blast of air. "Yeah, but I haven't updated my photo in, like, forever. What is she, a stalker or something? Who pays that much attention to detail? There were about, like, fifty people in the room that night. How could she have remembered *me*?"

Sam sighed. "What actually *did* you think of the book? I mean, you came along that night, but you didn't say anything after she left."

"I came because I always come. She, on the other hand, isn't one of us," I said in a flat tone.

"What do you mean by that?" There was an edge of disdain in Sam's voice, like they were mocking me.

"Nothing," I snapped. "I'm not a racist, if that's what you're thinking. I'm just saying that she isn't a regular. She doesn't come to our normal, monthly events."

"I know, she came because I invited her for Author Spotlight." There was a definite note of annoyance in Sam's voice that time; they couldn't hide it from me. "Listen, Michelle, what am I supposed to say back to her?"

"Tell her you don't know. How would you? We only see each other once a month at the open mics. How would you know what I think of her flippin' book; what are you, a mind reader? Do you even have a reader account?" My face flushed with heat as I waited for Sam's response.

Sam gave another sigh. "Alright, I'll tell her that I don't know, but that I'm sorry she had a negative experience after the event."

I made a sucking noise on my teeth. "Why should you tell her sorry? I'm just sorry that *she* put *you* in an awkward position and tried to turn us against each other."

***

NICKY

Unfortunately I can't say that I could have any insight on that matter as we didn't discuss it afterwards, and nor have we had any Author Spotlight slots before. But you could be correct in guessing that if an author was present it might make an opinion on a book less likely to occur and therefore I can see why you might have felt it was random and came out of the blue.

I reread the message, then once more, my eyes tripping over the letters. It was possibly the most awkwardly worded email I had ever received; loaded with double-triple negatives designed to deliberately confuse the meaning. In other words, the biggest excuse for a non-answer I had ever read. I was tempted to respond with a string of head-scratching emojis but thought better of any reactionary response. What did my gut feeling tell me about Sam's email?

That they knew Michelle didn't like my book – or indeed me – but were keeping it under wraps.

Sam and Michelle were friends; that much was obvious. Together with that other woman, the blonde called Lisa who had giggled with Michelle at my expense, all three of them – Lisa, Sam and Michelle –

had body language that hinted at a long-standing friendship group.

I sunk my chin onto my palm. There was nothing else for it, except to thank Sam for their response. I'd make sure not to bother ever going near *Bookish Buns* again, at least. If their literary circle acted like teenagers, then it was no place I wanted to have anything more to do with. I needed to make business relationships with people who were business-like in their conduct and took accountability for their actions.

Blech, what a fat load. As if I didn't already have more stacked against me in my career as a small-press author. It wasn't really any different to being an 'Indie' writer; I'd been down that route before with my first short-story collection that I self-published several years previously. I knew how hard it was to get your book out there in front of readers. I wasn't a big-name bestseller who had a PR team to promote my books and handle negative feedback; it was just me. My publisher, Janet, was a lovely person, but she was based in Edinburgh, at the other end of the UK, and therefore I hadn't physically met her; I very much felt alone in my publishing journey. I had needed to arrange my own signing event at a local bookstore, and even then, she had asked me to buy author copies from her, rather than supply them to the bookstore herself as she hadn't wanted to deal with their 50% retailer discount on the wholesale price. I had been left to foot that bill myself. Furthermore, after launching Dog Days of Doom at the start of July, and doing a few posts to announce it, she hadn't done much more to promote it other than posting a few promotional banners on the *Olive Branch Books* website and on their publisher social media accounts.

I really felt alone; and having a one-star rating from someone who had a personal grudge against me for reasons that were inexplicable to me, rather than about the merits of my book itself, really hurt. It stank and it hurt. Why me? What had I done to deserve it? A one-star rating could be the death of my book. What if people looked at it and thought there must be a problem with my book. It had certainly pulled my book's average rating down from 4.5 to 3.5 online; the sight of those stars, only half full, gave me a shudder.

Deep breath. I let the cold intake of air sooth my lungs and refresh my mind.

If Sam wasn't going to do anything to fix the issue, then I would have to reach out to Michelle myself; just to send a friendly message and hopefully find out what she didn't like about my book. I wouldn't ask her to change her rating; her opinion was her choice, but at least I would know *why* she disliked my book so much.

I searched for her name, 'Michelle Connor' and found her profile. She used the same photo for all her socials, so it was definitely her. My fingers hovered above the keypad and I started to type in a short message:

Hi Michelle. We didn't get a chance to meet at Bookish Buns last week. I saw that you left a rating for Dog Days of Doom online and wanted to thank you for sharing your feedback, even if the book wasn't to your liking. Obviously I would love readers to enjoy my book, so if you'd care to share why you didn't like it, I'd be grateful as this might help other readers like yourself. Thanks and appreciation, Nicky xx

I took a deep breath and hit send. Why on earth was my heart hammering in my chest? I reflected on that for a moment. Could it be that I felt like I was consorting with the enemy? Could be. It certainly felt disingenuous to offer thanks to someone who had left a one-star rating for my book. I personally had never – would never – leave a one-star rating of any book. I had an appreciation of how long it took for a book, even one not to my taste, to be written and edited. It took the best part of twelve months of blood, sweat and tears to produce a novel and I had an elementary respect for the author for going through that, even if their story wasn't my cup of tea. For this *woman* to carelessly toss one star at my book showed the utmost disrespect for me and utter contempt for my book. I found my top lip twitching upwards and consciously stopped the sneer that I knew was forming.

***

MICHELLE

Oh – my – God.

How had that crazy woman found out my profile?

I blinked at the tiny, smiling photo of the braided bitch and my eyes skittered over her poison words.

"Ugh," I sighed aloud. "Ugh! The cheek. Just ugh!"

"What is it? What are you tutting about?"

I jabbed a finger at my laptop. "Your favourite fancy-woman just got in contact with me. Can you believe that?"

I watched Ash's eyes travel left to right, dropping further down the page as she read the private message. The corner of her mouth jerked into a lopsided smile. "What's the problem with it?"

"What's the problem?" I nodded at the screen. "Stalker much?"

"She's not *stalking* you," said Ash in the pantomime voice she affected when she was mocking me. "She just wants to know why you don't like her book. It's fair enough, really."

"Oh yeah, take her side why don't you? Just cause you would love to get in her pants," I teased.

Ash rolled her eyes. "You're the only woman for me, even if you are a jealous cow."

"Joking aside, don't you think that's a touch passive aggressive? She's trying to bully me into giving her an answer. Why should I?"

Ash shrugged and I knew she was being deliberately blasé. "Don't reply, then."

"I won't. Awful woman gave me the creeps." I shuddered. "I'll do one better, in fact, and block her.

***

NICKY

I sat back in my chair feeling more relaxed. My message ought to do it. Most people were nice underneath; for all I knew Michelle might have even been having a bad day and simply took it out on my book. She would probably write back with a few words about what she didn't like, now that she could see I was kind and approachable. Hopefully the matter would be resolved soon.

I looked back at her profile. Further down her page were a few photos that had been set to public. A recent photo, from the 4th July showed Michelle sitting on an outdoor patio chair next to a woman with short, black hair that was dyed white-blonde at the front. Mousey-brown Michelle and her trendy-looking companion with black lipstick were shoulder to shoulder. They both wore alien t-shirts and waved small American flags in each hand. Michelle had a small lap-dog on her knee: a Yorkshire terrier. The caption below the photo read, 'Happy Independence Day, y'all. From the Burtons.'

So, that must have been Michelle's wife, and guessing from the display, her wife was American. Further down was a wedding photo showing Michelle in a 1940s style lace dress with squared shoulders and a pink sash and her bride wearing a black tuxedo complete with pink tie to match her sash. The caption read "I do!" Other public posts showed links for mental health organisations to help others access help when feeling suicidal and a few posts about a fundraiser to rescue dogs from puppy farms in China.

I closed the window on my phone. If Michelle was as nice as her public information made her out to be, then I was sure I would get a reasonable response from her.

***

MICHELLE

The house was silent. Well, all except for Ash snoring upstairs. I hadn't even managed to wake up Jaffa, who usually seemed to have a psychic knack for when I went for my nightly kitchen venture for a snack.

I yawned as I entered the kitchen and stubbed my toe on the pedal bin near the door. "Fiddlesticks!"

My laptop was on the kitchen counter where I had checked the fundraiser while drinking my Horlicks before bed. I flipped it open and minimised the window for *Save Dogs from Dinner Plates* and instead opened a new window for my reader account.

What if?

Yes. What if–

No. No what ifs. I would do it.

I removed my one-star rating of Nicky's book and signed out of my account with a smile. Next, I signed into Ash's account. We were an old married couple, we knew each other's logins for emails and all our socials.

I clicked on Nicky's profile and scrolled down to her book. It was the only one, her debut, so was easy to find. I marked the book as 'read' from Ash's account and clicked one star.

There. That would teach her to *snake* on me to Sam, and to harass me by private message. She wouldn't know the one star was associated with me as she hadn't met Ash at *Bookish Buns*. Not that Ash would ever read her book, or probably even care about what I had done anyway. Thrillers weren't her thing and apart from fancying the look of Nicky, I doubted Ash had given her much thought. I sniffed at the distasteful thought of my wife's crush. Not that I really believed Ash would ever cheat on me, but it wasn't exactly like Nicky and I were anything like the same type; I had porcelain skin and an angelic disposition, always helping others, whereas she was all darkness and grimness, her mind dwelling in dark thrillers and sordid crimes, the stuff she wrote about.

I was better than her for sure. I arched my back, satisfied that the horrible author had got what she deserved.

***

NICKY

Ash Burton. Who was Ash Burton?

The one-star rating under the name 'Ash Burton' glared back at me, as though the very essence of the screen on which it sat taunted me. Mind you, the timing was odd. I clicked on my book title, allowing the information to pop up for Dog Days of Doom. Only a single one-star rating had been added; that meant, Michelle Connor had removed her bad rating.

Ash Burton. The name was familiar. Where had I heard 'Burton' before?

A horrible, sinking feeling grabbed at my heart. Michelle Connor's profile page had shown a family photo entitled 'Happy Independence Day, y'all. From the Burtons.'

I searched for Michelle Connor's profile again to verify my deduction, but it was gone. Strange. I clicked on my web history and found the html for my search of her profile, then clicked on it.

Nothing.

Very strange. Did that mean Michelle Connor had blocked me from contacting her? Only one way to find out. I would ask Neil later.

I stared at the blank screen, my mind racing. If Ash Burton was Michelle Connor's wife, then did that mean Michelle had put her up to leaving a one-star rating for my book? What did Ash have against me; she hadn't even attended Bookish Buns during my event? I wasn't convinced it was mere coincidence; I had never received any one-star reviews before. What was going on?

Baffled, I clicked back on my author account. The least I could do in the meantime to protect myself was to block Ash Burton and Michelle Connor and report the abuse.

***

LISA

"You're shitting me, Michelle. Tell me you're shitting me." I stretched out on my front on my bed, holding the phone propped up in both hands and gawped at my bestie's face on the screen.

She shook her head. "Can you believe she did that? I mean, that's stalking, right? She must have searched for me online and DMed me. The bitch is bold as brass."

I waved my hand dismissively. "What a horrible cow. Like, I wouldn't even call her an author, she's such a nobody. Just so arrogant. Imagine stalking and harassing someone, the cheek of her. Did you block her?"

"You betcha I did. Imagine challenging me about my one-star rating. I'm entitled to my opinion, right?" Michelle puckered her face.

"Yeah-uh! It's a free country. Maybe not in Nigeria where that slag is from, but it sure is in England." I folded my arms.

"And can you believe that she *snaked* on me to Sam? Yeah, like, she apparently asked Sam if I'd given any feedback on the night. That's so high-school, isn't it?"

I harumphed, theatrically. "Oh-em-gee, like how immature can you get? She really did that?"

Michelle nodded, dipping her head with big, exaggerated gestures. "She even wanted me to write about why I gave it one star."

I could feel my blood boil. What made that bitch of a writer so entitled as to *demand* that people explain why they didn't like her book. A plan began to formulate in my mind. I couldn't let this slide. Two people close to me had been hurt: Sam no doubt felt bad as Nicky had been invited to *Bookish Buns* as Author Spotlight, and my lovely bestie Michelle felt awful because she had been stalked and harassed. Who would want some random stranger searching for them, especially when they were a crime writer? I mean, it was hard not to think that if Nicky had such a wicked, devious imagination as to write a story like *Dog Days of Doom*, what if she acted out some of those imaginary impulses in real life? Like stalking and murdering people?

I was outraged, and rightly so. Time for a revenge review for Nicky after what she had done to my bestie and my other friend. It was vigilante justice, just like the topic of her book. Or maybe poetic justice, if I wanted to be literary.

Michelle was a much better writer than Nicky anyway. I had read my bestie's short stories. Someday they would be published and by that time, everyone would have forgotten about Nicky Odelola and her wretched book, Dog Days of nothing.

***

NICKY

Not another bad rating.

The thumbnail photo next to the one-star rating showed a blonde-haired woman with the name Lisa Thomas. The bad rating also had a short review. My eyes skimmed the text:

I really wanted to like this book, and I thought it had a quirky style, but it didn't work for me. The concept of the Black Dog was too far-fetched and the main characters weren't realistic. The dialogue was stilted and unnatural and not like people speak in this city. Disappointing.

There was no way it was a legitimate review, given the timing, which was strange. I had gone from having no bad ratings to three within the space of two days, all within a week of my Author Spotlight event. Then there was the issue of the name. Lisa. Wasn't that the name of the blonde-haired woman in the audience who Sam had specifically called out for giggling during my talk? Yes; Lisa Thomas who was friends with Michelle Connor, the perpetrator of my other one-star troll rating. This was a deliberate attack; this was personal.

My appetite for my marmalade and toast had gone. In fact, it was as though my stomach had bottomed out. I was starting to dread checking into any sites where my book was listed for fear of another troll rating being posted. Had Michelle Connor put her friend, Lisa Thomas up to this latest attack on me? Yes, there was no denying this was the same Lisa, Michelle's friend, from Bookish Buns. The middle-aged blonde who had dressed vaguely witchy, with her pentagram necklace and glittery black bohemian skirt. Gosh, what next? Was she going to cast a spell on me too?

What had I done to either of them? I was simply a small-press author trying to get a foothold.

Time to take action. I didn't have to be at my day job at the library on High Street until eleven o'clock. I would go down to Bookish Buns café and talk things out with Sam, and maybe try to nip things in the bud with Michelle and Lisa lest they escalate; which I feared they would.

***

LISA

A bad review wasn't enough.

No, that wouldn't be enough to put a narcissist like Nicky Odelola in her place. I had to think outside the box; think bigger than simply posting a revenge rating online. Soon, the bitch would be asking me to change my review. She was full-of-herself; of course she would.

The ping of a notification alerted me to a message. I clicked to read the note:

Hi Lisa. We didn't get a chance to meet at Bookish Buns last week. I saw that you left a review for Dog Days of Doom online and wanted to thank you for sharing your feedback, even if the book wasn't to your liking. I'm grateful that you cared to post your thoughts. Thanks and appreciation, Nicky xx

So – fucking – predictable. I almost clapped myself on the back at my ability to predict that such a message would be waiting for me.

Wait til Michelle heard about this. She was *so* right about Nicky being a stalker. Clearly, Nicky had looked me up too if she'd managed to find my profile. It would take something more than a bad review to make the bitch back off, when she'd latched onto all of us – Sam, Michelle, and me – so hard.

Maybe something stronger in the form of black magic.

I rubbed my pentagram necklace; hopefully it would instill a dose of inspiration. I could always cast a spell on her; maybe a hex to make her come down with a bout of shingles, or swine flu, or another lurgy that would knock her off her feet for a while. Would that be satisfying? Not really. How would I get to see the results of my hard work if she was holed up in bed, instead of running around town, her face twisted in fear. No; it had to be a punishment with much more visual consequences so that I could enjoy the consequences she'd been subjected to.

A better idea came to mind; like a light-bulb switching on, it cast a bright glow in my mind. I would take a leaf out of Nicky's own book, Dog Days of Doom, and inflict a punishment on her that would remind her of what she had written for her own characters. I rubbed my hands together in celebration of my fiendishly devious plan. Oh, I was so clever. Too clever for that bitch. I would teach her a subliminal lesson that she deserved and make her paranoid that someone was out there in the shadows, watching her and waiting to deliver a comeuppance for stalking poor Michelle, my bestie.

***

NICKY

This was going too far.

I looked at the effigy on the front door mat. It was the figurine of a woman made out of black wax; I could tell that much from the two lumps on the torso, that seemed to resemble crude breasts. It had a rounded stump of a head, two arms and two legs, but no facial features or even hands and feet.

Who would do such a repulsive thing? I looked left and then right, both ways along the quiet, leafy street. Apart from our regular postman slipping in and out of the neighbours' gardens while he did his morning rounds, there was a middle-aged man walking a dog and an older lady jogging in Lycra while listening to earphones. None of the three of them looked to be a suitable culprit.

The effigy hadn't been there when I had dropped Nevaeh to school. Did that mean someone had been watching my house. Such a notion made my heart race with fear. First of all, that meant a hostile person had found out where I lived. Second of all, they must have been watching to see when I would return and put the figurine there while I was inside, knowing I would soon discover it. Third, and worst of all, whoever the person was must have harboured such a grudge against me as to put such a dreadful thing on my doorstep.

Was it a golliwog? I stooped and picked the object up. Attached to the wax head were three crinkled hairs. My hairs; stray hairs. The blood in my veins turned tepid at the sight.

I stepped back inside my house and slammed the door shut, then peeked out the side panel window. It had to be one of the trolls from Bookish Buns. Sam? Unlikely. Michelle? Maybe, though she seemed more histrionic by blocking me and getting her wife to leave a bad review of my book online. Who then? Lisa. Yes; witchy Lisa. She might have even cast a spell on the doll, using that awful pentagram necklace of hers. She seemed like a jealous, vindictive sort. I recalled how she had monopolised all the attention in the room that night while telling an anecdote about her hometown. She clearly disliked anyone else being the central focus, so that could potentially be a motivating factor if she was the culprit behind the creepy doll. I shivered, thinking of her trawling my chair for stray hairs on the fabric, then going to the trouble of melting them into the wax effigy. Only a deranged person would think of such a thing.

Wait a moment; *I myself* had thought of such a thing, hadn't I? In my book, granted, not in real life. In Dog Days of Doom, my central Black Dog character left a calling card to the small business owners he targeted. He left small, black plastic dog models on their doorsteps as a sinister signal that they were being watched.

I was being trolled. They had copied the plot from my own book.

***

MICHELLE

One hundred and fifty pounds had been raised for *Save dogs from dinner plates.* My heart swelled as I looked at my laptop screen. Money to be well spent helping to get more dogs out of cages and across to Korea. I gave Jaffa a celebratory hug, then set her down to drink water from the bowl under my table.

The tinkling of the wind chimes announced the front door of Bookish Buns opening. I looked up from my charity fundraiser and immediately wanted to shrink in my seat as none other than the stalker-author Nicky Odelola herself walked in.

What the hell did she want? I ducked down and peered over the top of my laptop. Was she here to complain about the bad ratings for her book? If so, two could play at that game. I had as much cause to complain as she did; stalking was a crime, and so was cyber harassment, and that awful woman had done both to me by searching for me and contacting me online.

Didn't seem like she had seen me. Lucky for me I had chosen to sit further back in the corner, partially hidden by a shelf full of pre-loved books that Sam had curated for customers to read while they ate her delicious culinary treats. How fun for me to be able to watch the exchange play out between Sam and her without the horrible author knowing. As much as I strained my ears to listen, I couldn't hear a word. Not to worry; I would find out all the gossip from Sam later.

Looked like it was a serious exchange, judging by the expressions on both their faces. Nicky gesticulated with her hands up. So, she was playing innocent, huh? Devious cow. Bet she was playing the victim to Sam, to get her sympathy. Probably making me look to be a psycho too for giving her a one-star rating. And what was that she was showing Sam? She held something too small for me to make out in the palm of her hand. Sam didn't seem to know what it was either, as they shook their head and shrugged. Whatever had happened was clearly not the reaction that Nicky wanted, for she dropped whatever it was in the bin by the counter, turned and left the café.

This was too juicy for me to wait. I tugged Jaffa's leash, and we approached the front counter where poor Sam stood, looking rather dejected.

"What was all that?" I said.

Sam looked out the door at the street beyond, their eyes darting among the passersby, no doubt looking for Nicky.

"Nothing," Sam answered.

"You know, what she's doing is bullying and harassment. We'd be within our rights to contact the police and have her banned," I added.

Sam looked appalled. "That's going a bit far. I think it's all sorted now, anyway. I highly doubt she'll be back."

"You never can tell with a psycho like that," I sniffed.

Sam sighed. "I really don't need all this, honestly."

"Well, just let me know if there's anything I can do to help." I reached out and rubbed their arm.

They seemed to bristle under my touch and pull back their arm. "No, that's okay. You've done enough already."

Jaffa tugging on the lead distracted me. My dog was snuffling at something in the bin. "Get out of there, you silly moo!"

I pulled my pet out of the bin, though it took quite an effort. Whatever had attracted her attention sure was appealing. Jaffa strained to keep nosing at whatever it was, and licked crumbs off her nose.

"I'd better get this one home, I don't know what's got her so fidgety. I'll see you on Thursday at the next open mic. I've finally finished my story, so I'll be reading it. Ash checked it for me and gives it a double thumbs up, so you're in for a treat."

***

LISA

It was too funny. Just so fucking funny!

I couldn't stop laughing at the sight of Nicky stomping out of Bookish Buns. Her tantrum had been divine to watch. Simply heavenly. I was able to watch the whole spectacle from my car parked across the street. The dumb bitch had been waving my wax doll around in her hand too; I'd seen her throw it into the bin before she left. Poor Sam had taken the brunt of Nicky's wrath though; I'd make it up to them later.

Wonder who Nicky had accused of leaving the doll on her doorstep: me, or Michelle? If she had half a brain, she would know that I was behind it, dark-magic Lisa, not innocent, Snow Angel-loving Michelle. Even less than half a brain once the oleander I'd coated the doll with had time to sink through her skin. What did oleander do? Let's see: blurred vision for one. Then there was heart palpitations, not to mention hallucinations and coming down with a cold sweat. Probably the shits too. Of course, with a strong enough dose, there were also the three Cs: coughing fits, convulsions and finally coma. The dose I'd given her was weaker; the bitch wasn't worth going to jail over. But it was strong enough for a good dose of entertainment, and that was why I'd done it.

Nicky had only just disappeared out of sight in the crowd further along the street, when the door of Bookish Buns opened again and this time Michelle stepped out, with Jaffa trailing behind on her lead. I quickly jumped out of my car.

"Hey BF," I said.

Michelle's face broke into a delighted grin. "Aww, bestie, you missed all the drama. You'll never guess who was just in the café."

"I know, I saw her leave. What did Nicky want?"

As if I didn't know. Michelle would be thrilled when I told her about the wickedly genius punishment I had inflicted upon Nicky. But I would get to it soon. It would be the icing on the cake after she told me all the devious details of Nicky's complaint to Sam first. All in good time.

"Sam wouldn't tell me. I'm guessing it was to complain about the bad ratings about her book," said Michelle, with a half-shrug of one shoulder.

I opened my mouth, about to share my fiendishly fantastic punishment, when Jaffa started gagging. The dog's body convulsed as it arched its back, hacking and spluttering, like it was yakking on a bone.

"Jaffa, what did you eat, you silly na-na," Michelle patted the dog on its back, but it continued coughing and gagging.

"Is she going to be sick?" I said.

The dog was wheezing, and convulsing.

"I hope she didn't eat chocolate, it's poisonous for dogs. She was nosing around in the bin when I was talking to Sam on the way out."

Michelle's words sank through me like a lead balloon. The oleander-soaked wax doll was in the bin. I had seen Nicky, through the glass fronted café, as she had thrown it into the bin in a huge strop.

"Sam doesn't use chocolate, as it's a dog-friendly café," I reassured. But who would reassure me? How could I admit to Michelle about the wax doll now, especially if, by chance, Jaffa got worse as a result of my handiwork? Not that I had brought my wax dolly to Sam's café, of course; that had been Nicky's decision, and therefore her fault.

As Jaffa began shaking, her eyes bulging, and Michelle's cries for help filled my ears, there was only one thing I could do. I bundled both of them in my car. "We have to get her over to the vet. I suspect that Nicky has poisoned your dog."

***

NICKY

I took a sip of Pinot Noir – a big sip – and let the alcohol wash away my anxiety. Liquid medicine, once in a while, was good for the soul.

It had gone badly at Bookish Buns. Certainly worse than what I was hoping for. Sam had no accountability for an event that *they* had organised. Their reaction was to act like anything that happened going forwards was nothing to do with them. Even after I had described the three one-star ratings and Lisa's bad review. Even after I had shown the wax golliwog.

"It's an event that's open to the public, so I have no control over what people might do afterwards," they had said.

"But they're your friends. Can't you talk to them?" I had said.

"I only see them once a month at the open mic events, and we don't discuss any readings afterwards. We didn't discuss your event," they had continued.

"You invited me as Author Spotlight, though. I thought as the host you would've made sure it was a receptive audience," I had said. "But instead the harassment got worse, after the event. One of them left this on my doorstep."

I had shown Sam the golliwog and watched their face stare blankly at it.

"I don't know anything about that," came the response.

And that was that. All I could do was respond to whatever came next. If it escalated, I would have to involve the police. What I badly wanted was for it all to go away – it was a waking nightmare. At least that hideous, creepy doll had been dumped in the bin at Bookish Buns. Sam could take that out with the rest of the rubbish that they cultivated at their café.

***

MICHELLE

"I kidd you not, the crazy bitch tried to poison my sweet Jaffa."

I nodded to emphasise my point as I scoured all the shocked faces in Bookish Buns.

"But why would she feed a voodoo doll to your dog?" a woman, who I recognised from the open mic nights asked.

"She's a crime writer, isn't she? I'll bet she thought it was a clever way to get back at me for giving her a one-star rating and then blocking her when she tried to contact me about it. Maybe she's a psycho, for all I know. Only a psycho would do something like that – to give bad juju to an innocent dog."

"Is Jaffa okay?" said newbie Sara, her face aghast.

"Thankfully, yes. But I had to pay eight hundred quid for the vet bill as my insurance didn't cover the fifteen hundred total. She needed surgery to remove the evil thing, it was stuck in her intestines," I said. "She's resting at my mum's while I get my payback."

"What are you going to do?" said Sam.

"I'm going to march over to her house and post a bill for eight hundred quid through her letterbox for the hurt she caused to my dog. If she doesn't agree to pay it, I might take legal action against her."

Lisa squirmed in her seat. "Isn't that going a bit far? I mean, what's the proof that she deliberately tried to hurt your dog? What if she meant to put the doll in this café as a curse, but not to specifically target Jaffa?"

I gritted my teeth. "She put the voodoo doll in the bin, so of course she knew Jaffa would eat it. It was on purpose, to get back at me. I'm sure of it."

"But she didn't even know you were here. She came to see me, and said the doll had been left on her doorstep," said Sam.

I couldn't believe my ears; why was Sam – and Lisa – sticking up for Nicky?

"That must've been part of her sneaky plot, don't you see? She made the voodoo doll of me, brought it to the café pretending someone else gave it as a curse to her, then dropped it in the bin knowing that I come here all the time with Jaffa. You see? It was to get revenge on me," I shouted.

Enough was enough. If they weren't going to believe me, then I would seek justice all by myself. I stood up, sending my chair skidding backwards.

"Wait for me, bestie. If you're going to her house, I'll come too," said Lisa.

Good; I was glad my BF had seen sense. I was right, and I was justified. Nicky would pay for her malicious crime against me, and my beloved pet.

***

LISA

A tremor of excitement rocked my body as I watched Michelle spray paint large blue letters on Nicky's front door. The slogan 'Dog killer' was displayed in capital letters diagonally. Maybe it was the anarchy of the moment that stopped me from admitting that I had given the wax doll to Nicky, not Nicky to Jaffa.

I hadn't had fun like that since I'd been to Michelle's hen party, before she got married to Ash three years ago, and we'd been so drunk that we'd all ended up in the fountain in the town square. Someone had called the peelers that night and we'd all legged-it back to our hotel. This time, I had that same sensation of fun; it was liberating to be part of a group of middle-aged women acting like adolescents. Don't ask me why. Maybe it was the spontaneity of the moment. It wasn't every day that I got to be part of a spur-of-the-moment act that wasn't *entirely* legal. Okay, if I was being honest, illegal. But I was only being honest to myself. Not to anyone else. Keeping it to myself was okay.

Where would the fun stop, though? Another tremor of excitement rippled through me at the notion of what level we would take it to next. After bad reviews, cursed dolls and spray paint, what would serve as a continuation of the payback we were inflicting on Nicky Odelola for her arrogance?

***

NICKY

"Hello, 999. What's your emergency?"

"Um, hello. I'm under attack. There is a hostile group of women with dogs on choke-chains outside my house. They're spray-painting my front door at the moment and banging on the windows. I think they're trying to get inside. The dogs are barking aggressively."

"Okay madam. Can you tell me if any of them are inside your property?"

I sighed, listening to the 999 call handler. "Not yet. But they're trying to bust down my door. I'm on my own as my husband is at work and my daughter's at school and I'm afraid of what they might do if they get me. They've been targeting me for a couple of weeks now and it's escalating. I think it's a racist attack, they sent me a wax golliwog made with some of my hairs as a warning, I can't think of any other reason why they're doing this. They don't know me."

"Madam, could you give me your address? We will send a patrol car around to your property."

Another sigh of relief. "So you think it might be a hate crime?"

"We will get an officer to come round and assess the situation."

Good. Hopefully the police would come soon and arrest them all. Vicious bunch of bitches. What had I done to them?

I gave my details to the call handler. As my life wasn't under immediate threat, she ended the call, with the assurance that a patrol car was in the area and would be there soon. With the fear in my heart eased, a notch anyway, I dared to peer out the living room window. Michelle Connor was among the throng, holding a can of blue paint in her hand. The blonde wannabe-witch, Lisa, stood back a little, a wide grin on her face which was clear even in the shade cast by her wide-brimmed black hat. The other women and dogs in their group trampled my nasturtiums and pansies, wrecking my garden.

Lisa's eyes turned to the gap in my net curtain and made eye contact with me. I dropped the curtain into place, my breath catching in my throat. She tugged on Michelle's jacket, alerting her friend's attention to that fact that I was home. Had they thought my house empty while they defaced it?

Just then, red and blue lights signalled the arrival of the police car. The women and their dogs scattered, stampeding towards my gate. Beyond the hedge at the bottom of my garden was a flight of concrete stairs and a narrow hand railing, that led towards the main road below where Nevaeh's school and the shops beyond lay. With the police car blocking the way out of the cul-de-sac that was my street, they all charged towards the single flight of stairs. Lisa was in the lead, one hand on her witchy-hat as she ran. Michelle followed her friend, brandishing the can of blue paint in her hand as she waddled along after her friend. Another of their friends dashed next, pulled by her pug on its leash.

I heard a scream, followed by several more. I stood on my tiptoes, straining to see over the hedge. No use; I dashed upstairs to look out the bedroom window.

Two police officers loitered until they heard the scream, then pursued the group down the stairs; I couldn't see Lisa, or Michelle, as they had been at the front of the group. Who had screamed? Curiosity overcame me. I went back downstairs, out my front door, out of my garden in my slippers and onto the street to see.

***

MICHELLE

It happened so fast. My life had flashed before my eyes as the world sped by. At least, I think it did. Must've been mere seconds before I had blacked out.

Lisa had been ahead of me, her blonde hair streaming back across her shoulders as she ran, holding one hand on her hat. I knew the police were behind us; maybe that was why I had panicked. I had dropped the spray can, and it had bounced onto the step in front of my bestie. Her foot had slipped on it. Her legs had arced in front and both arms had flown upwards. With her black dress resembling wings and her pointed hat a sharp beak, she had been as a raven taking flight.

A knock-on effect had spiralled from there. A pug had come out of nowhere, dashing in front of me and tripping me with its leash. I had fallen forwards, unlike Lisa, tumbling headlong down the concrete steps. Maybe that was why I'd ended up unconscious, whereas Lisa had remained awake to her pain.

Every part of my body ached. Was I lucky that because I had been knocked out, my body had gone floppy, saving me from greater injuries? A broken ankle wasn't as serious as it could have been. My thoughts jumped to the voodoo doll that had been pulled from Jaffa's intestines; it had been intact apart from its right foot, which hung at a ninety degree angle by a single hair – one of Nicky's. Apparently my right ankle had been sticking out at a ninety degree angle to the rest of my leg, when the ambulance crew had moved me from the bottom of the steps onto a gurney. I shivered at the thought of the curse Nicky had put on me. All I could do was hope that now the curse had been fulfilled, the rest of the bad energy had dissipated into the ether and the evil bitch could do me no more harm.

"Michelle." Ash appeared in the bedroom doorway, rousing me from my daydreams. I pushed myself into a sitting position in our double bed, greeting her with a huge grin. She didn't return it.

"Is something wrong, hun?" I said.

"Yes. I just signed into my reader account. Did you post a one-star rating of Adenike's book, Dog Days of Doom, from my account?"

I lowered my eyes as I nodded. There was no point denying it.

"Do you know how I found out?" she went on.

I shook my head, my eyes still lowered.

"Because the police told me. They're investigating the harassment of that author as a potential hate crime. Why on earth did you involve me?"

I stared at my wife, but couldn't bring myself to answer.

"Well? Could you at least do me the courtesy of answering? Don't you realise the trouble I could get into if I'm painted as a racist because of something that *you* did behind my back? I work in a multicultural school, for crying out loud. Half the teenagers I work with are from black and minority ethnic backgrounds."

I put up both my hands. "I'm sorry. I didn't think of that."

"No, you didn't think at all. Harassing her from my account, spray painting her house – are you having a nervous breakdown?" Ash's face was crumpled with anger.

"She nearly killed Jaffa. She tricked her into eating a voodoo doll that she made of me – an effigy to put a curse on me. I had to do something," I said, my palms still turned over in protest.

"Correction – your friend Lisa made that wax thing apparently to scare Adenike. The police told me. She'd confessed to it."

My jaw dropped. "There's no way my bestie did that. Lisa would've told me. It's that Nicky woman. She's put a curse on the police to make them believe her."

"What on earth are you *on* about?"

I flapped my hands, ignoring my wife. "Or maybe she even put a curse on Lisa to make her give a false confession. Yeah, that must be what happened."

"Are you even listening to yourself?" Ash's mouth hung open.

I folded my arms. "I don't believe it – and I won't – unless Lisa tells me she did it. It's more likely that Nicky did it. Voodoo is from her culture, not ours."

Ash closed her eyes, shaking her head softly. I had never seen such a look of disgust on her face.

"I'm going to stay at my mum's. I need to space to think. Don't come over to collect Jaffa – I'll keep her with me. She needs someone responsible to take care of her."

***

LISA

Why was the green mother angry at me? I hadn't done anything wrong.

For the mother to be angry at one of her green witches meant I had created an imbalance somehow. I couldn't see how. I had only delivered what had been deserved; Nicky had harassed my BF, so I had harassed her in turn with the wax doll. And it had been Michelle, not me, who had spray-painted Nicky's house. So, why had the can slipped under *my* feet, causing *me* to fall down the stairs? Not any of the other women, with their angry dogs. Me, who had stood in the background, a watcher.

Unlike Michelle, who had been knocked out, I had been awake throughout my suffering. I had three fractured ribs. I had dislocated my left hip. I had broken my right wrist. The hospital staff had said, in so many words, that my voluptuous curves had protected my internal organs from injuries but had caused more injuries overall because I had fallen harder, and landed more heavily, than a skinny bitch would have.

Sometimes the green mother worked in mysterious – and incomprehensible – ways. Okay, maybe not so incomprehensible. I had been kicked out of the *Circle* back in March, for hexing a *tart* during Ostara – but only because she deserved it. She started dating the man that *I* had set my sights on. He would've preferred *me*, not that plain skank, so she had it coming.

***

NICKY

What a relief the police were investigating all the harassment and taking it seriously as a potential hate crime. Could that really be why all of it – the bad ratings, the wax golliwog, the spray-paint – had happened? Not because they were jealous of my author career, but because they were racist.

A combination of both, more likely.

Still, how ironic that, just as dogs had been the common thread throughout my novel, dogs had been the central theme of payback in my real-life harassment. Dog Days of Doom: I had heard the police laughing about how a dog leash had tripped Michelle and caused her fall after targeting my house. Dog Days of Doom: her dog had eaten a wax effigy sent as a threat to me by her very own best friend.

Dog Days of Doom. A black dog had featured as the villain in my own crime novel. Michelle and Lisa had been the black dogs in my own crime tale. But I was free of them now. My own dog days of summer would be much better, now, free of the people who sought to hurt me.

A new title for another book popped into my head. It would be a crime novel like my debut, but this time based on my recent sinister experiences at the hands of wannabe-witch Lisa and cherub loving weirdo Michelle. My second novel: The Doghouse Duo.

The best revenge for a crime writer? Killing them in my next book.

Three

A Signature Look

Savannah took a sip of coffee and looked over the top of her computer. Why was focusing on her work so hard? Maybe it was nothing more than Monday blues; she hadn't yet got her head in gear. Or maybe she hadn't had enough caffeine. Yep, that was a more likely explanation.

She wasn't a fan of her new office, to be honest. It felt like she'd been pigeonholed. Was that a subliminal message from the company that she was a second-class worker; that her role was far less important than others?

As if being a Benefits Consultant was unimportant work. Heck, their branch wouldn't run properly if it weren't for her contribution. She glowered at her screen, all too aware of the second-class furniture she had been given in her office-downsize. Her swivel chair had a dodgy backrest that didn't stay in an upright position when she leaned against it and the computer wasn't at eye level. With a job that required being at her desk, in front of a computer, for eight hours a day, having ergonomic furniture was essential. She didn't want to get neck strain, or carpal tunnel syndrome.

A breeze flowed in as the door opened; already distracted, it didn't take much to make her look up from her screen.

A young man strode into the room. A few years younger than her at any rate; maybe late-twenties. He was on the smaller side for a bloke, maybe five foot eight, and had closely cropped, white-blonde hair and a goatee. With his silvery hair and pale skin, his deep-set, light blue eyes gave him an intense gaze as he strode closer to her.

Savannah spun in her chair to face him, as it seemed he intended to approach her. Without a word, the man passed by behind her chair, averting his eyes from hers at the last second. The air flow whipped up by his definite stride sent a shiver down her back and the overpowering scent of cologne almost made her sneeze. He walked to the other end of her office and turned into a door on the left.

That was odd. She hadn't met the guy, yet he didn't try to introduce himself, or even offer a smile or nod of hello. Nor did he offer an apology for walking through her office. Who did something like that? She bristled at the notion. Not very polite; she would never barge into a colleague's office without knocking and offering a polite greeting.

Come to think of it, he didn't dress like someone who worked in an office. His casual attire wasn't very businesslike; he wore a black tracksuit with white stripes down the side of each leg, and bright yellow trainers. The colour coordination of his clothing, together with his intense expression, gave her the impression of an angry bee. She smirked to herself; the image was going to be hard to forget.

***

Stay positive and make it happen.

Savannah tacked the laminated poster on the wall and stood back to admire it. She glanced at the three other posters, tacked on each wall: *Happiness starts with a smile; Make a change starting with your mindset* and *Live in the moment.*

It wasn't much, but it was a start. What her office could do with, honestly, was a new paint job. The yellow walls had long since faded to a sickly cream colour and there were marks where posters had been removed by whoever had been in there before her. Who had that been? She wracked her brain but couldn't recall. Her previous office had been down the other end of the building, in the newly renovated part. Until now, she'd had no reason to be in this old section of the building. Her previous office had been bright, airy and surrounded by people; she had never failed to find colleagues to chat to over a coffee as they passed the time, and it had made the day much more bearable and fun. But now?

Her door opened, and the tracksuit-clad man walked in. Instead of fixing her with his intense gaze, his focus dropped to her camel-coloured peep-toe stilettos. As with the previous day, the bloke didn't say a thing and strode past her, in a wind of cologne, and disappeared into the door at the other end of the room.

What was her office, a corridor? Savannah tossed her head. She had been half tempted to say it aloud for him to overhear. Or maybe she would say it as 'banter' the next time he came through. Such a joke might lighten the mood between them, especially since it now felt awkward for any introductions to be made. What was the etiquette on that anyway? She didn't know. All she *did* know was that he had passed through her current office twice without any attempt to speak to her. Not to mention the fact that the bloke radiated angry energy, making it harder to initiate any small talk.

***

Savannah.

Where was that name from? Where was SHE from, matter of fact? She looked Asian, had a bit of a Chinese look about her eyes, but then she was quite dark skinned. Sorta mocha coloured. Thai? Malaysian?

Small too. Most women were as tall as he was. She was small, like Carly. Carly was small and curvy. He glanced at their photo on the lock-screen of his phone; both wearing matching Santa hats, in front of the Eiffel tower. Carly held her right hat, ungloved, up at the camera showing her diamond ring.

Savannah was there when he opened the door. She looked up, large brown eyes peering up at him. Coy too, over her right shoulder. Moving the desk against the wall, before she got moved into the office, made the most sense as it gave him a clear path to his office on the other side, but now it had another purpose, causing her to look up every time he walked in. Fringe benefits. He smirked to himself as he sauntered into his office then, with the door firmly shut, let out a low whistle.

***

As the door at the far end of her office slammed, Savannah couldn't help but jump in her seat. What was with that?

"Take the door off the hinges next time, why don't you, asshole?" she muttered. "Bloody savage."

Saying it aloud was cathartic, even if it was so quiet that Angry Bee couldn't possibly have heard her.

As if in solidarity, her poster reading *Stay positive and make it happen* fell off the wall in protest. Either Angry Bee had banged his door so hard that the reverberation had knocked it off, or she hadn't blu-tacked it on well enough. She picked the laminated sheet up and stood up to fix it back onto the wall, giving a heavy thud from her fist, just for added measure since he was in the room next door.

***

S for Savannah.

S, the way her calf curved in those sand-coloured, high heeled shoes and dipped inward at the ankle.

S, for Savannah standing. S, the shape of the dip in her back and the curve of her ass. S for ass.

She was wearing sand-coloured leggings that matched her sand-coloured high heels. S for sand-coloured. He looked at the strip of smooth, tanned skin that was exposed at her waist as her shirt lifted upwards as she stretched to stick the boring platitude of a poster on the wall. 'Stay positive and make it happen'. Whatever made her tick.

1. *Those high heels would look good on Carly. Carly was heavier than Savannah though, but he could bet she would suit those shoes.*

Savannah had toffee-coloured highlights in her waist-length, dark hair. Bet Carly would look good with highlights too. Carly's long, curly black hair was natural though. Bet she'd also flip her lid if he asked her to dye it.

Which he would anyway. What was to stop him?

***

Why was her computer malfunctioning?

These things seemed to always happen on a Monday, just in time to make her life more difficult. Savannah sighed. Maybe it was a sign that she needed to go and make a coffee and find the nearest colleague to stop for a pick-me-up chat.

Yes, such a notion sounded like a great plan. She needed something to lift her mood after a weekend alone, watching romcoms, with her cats. Not that *Puss* and *Boots* weren't great company, of course. They never let her down. They never strung her along on a bunch of Swipe-right dates, acted with no affection and then dumped her.

Savannah's reflection in the black, blank computer screen looked pitiable. Her slumped, rounded shoulders gave the impression of someone who was seriously in need of a hug. Was she really that bad?

Fine. She had made up her mind. A lovely, fruit scone to go with that coffee. Or better still, those salted peanut chocolate covered domes that Jackie had brought in last week. If there were any of those still lurking around, she would devour them – easily. What were they called, anyway? She would need to find out, then buy all the stock from the convenience store across the road.

She stood up in a flurry, just as her office door swung open, causing her to collide with a tense, solid, someone that bounded in. Said tense, solid body belonged to none other than Angry Bee.

"Oh, I'm so sorry," she said, by way of reflex.

"Lo," came the curt response.

Lo, as in, hello? What sort of thing was that to say?

Without any apology, or any other comment at all, Angry Bee arced away from her then strode on through her office. Mind you, he was less 'Angry Bee' and more 'Blue Tang', what with his blue and black tracksuit combo with yellow trainers.

Whatever. Angry Bee or Blue Tang, she was starting to think the bloke was a *knob.* Why didn't he speak? And what was with the intense eye contact, giving her a *Village of the Damned* impression?

Well, she certainly wouldn't be looking to have a coffee and scone break with *him* for sure. Savannah glided out and made for the staff kitchen just as he disappeared through the mystery door at the other end of her office.

Kettle on, scone on a plate. Heck, she was in such dire need of comfort food that she would have eaten a week-old-hard-as-a-rock scone. Luckily a considerate somebody had covered it with cling film, meaning it had most likely survived the weekend with most of its freshness intact. She munched on it and let the hiss of the kettle lull her into a smooth calm.

A blue flash in the shiny silver of the kettle alerted her to a lingering presence behind. Savannah spun round in time to see that Angry Bee had entered the kitchen holding a small lunchbox. He opened the microwave and slotted his tub inside, but instead of focussing on his food, she noticed his eyes on her in the reflection of the microwave glass.

Who ate their lunch at half-past nine in the morning, anyway? She turned back to the kettle and poured a mug of tea, using the silvery side to spy on Angry Bee. He now had his back to the microwave, his tracksuit-clad arms folded across his chest, scowling at her while his food cooked.

Savannah shuddered; his gaze was starting to give her the creeps. Not just the fact that he watched her with such unbroken, intense eye contact, but the fact that he made no effort to talk. What was his deal? What did he even *do*?

***

Plug out, thirty seconds wait, plug in, switch on.

No response.

What was the deal with her computer? It was definitely her same old trusty PC that had been moved across from her previous office. Her bright, airy, spacious office that had privacy from strange colleagues strutting in and out and using it as a corridor.

Savannah ground her molars at the thought; the crunching sound of her molars wouldn't win her any points with her dentist.

"Need a hand?"

She jumped at the unexpected intrusion. Angry Bee was standing behind her. He was wearing a red tracksuit, zipped high to the collar, with black and white piping on the seams and bright green trainers to match. Or rather, to strain her eye. Who matched such colours together, it was so garish.

"Um, erm, it's fine. I'm just having computer trouble." Savannah tucked her hair behind her ear and cleared her throat.

Angry Bee leaned behind the computer. He grabbed a blue cable in the back of the machine and showed it to her. "There's your problem. The cable was unplugged."

Her nostrils flared; he had completely disregarded her dismissal of help. She looked at the tip of the cable between his fingers. It had a clear plastic connector with edges that flared out, so that it seemed if you plugged it into a USB port, it wouldn't be easily pulled out. How could such a device have got unplugged? The design seemed to have the sole purpose of keeping it attached to the computer; not that she knew much about PCs in the first place, of course. She relaxed. Angry Bee had proved useful; maybe she could learn to forgive him for unapologetically treating her office as a corridor, if he helped out in other areas.

***

Come on, this had to be a joke.

Another day, another IT issue. Savannah sipped her skinny latte and tried a second time to input her password. Same error message.

"Oh my freaking gosh, why is this happening to me?" She ran both hands through her hair.

She had definitely put the password in correctly, so what was causing the issue? Maybe it was a Monday morning thing; maybe the system had done an upgrade over the weekend. That would explain why things always went belly up at the start of the following week. Last week, it was an unplugged cable. This week, a password issue.

She took a deep breath, exhaled, and typed in her password again.

Another message appeared on the screen, informing her that since she had used the incorrect password three times, she was locked out of the system and would need IT support to reset it.

"You've got to be fucking kidding me?"

Thankfully she was logged into her emails on her phone, so she could at least manage to send a quick message to IT. She opened a new message.

To: IT Support
Subject: New password request
Hi ...

Come to think of it, who was the new IT support person? The last guy, James, had taken a promotion as IT manager at a rival firm. Who had replaced him?

Oh well, she didn't know. She would have to use a generic greeting instead.

Good morning,

I entered my password wrong on my computer this morning and it has locked me out of the system. Could you please reset it for me?

Thank you,
Savannah.

There wasn't much she could do without her computer, as she didn't have access to the spreadsheets on her phone since they contained sensitive client details, so it was a good excuse for a biscuit.

She was in the staff kitchen, when her phone buzzed. The IT support person had replied.

Hi Savannah

Have reset it to PASSWORD1 for u. If u have any other issues let me know and will stop by.

Vicky

Vicky. As in Victoria? Also, what was with the casual, 'text-speak' of how she wrote her words? Savannah went back to her office, biscuit in hand, and logged into her computer, using PASSWORD1. Sure enough, it booted up.

Not bad. This Vicky woman was very efficient at her job.

The door at the far end of her office opened and Angry Bee breezed into the room. Instead of striding past in his usual, intense manner, he stopped alongside Savannah's desk.

"Get sorted then?"

She looked up at him, momentarily disoriented by the intrusion. "Erm, sorted?"

His eyebrow went up. "You had problems logging in. I sent you the new password. Password 1, all caps? You should change that, by the way."

Savannah stared at him, his words connecting with her brain. "Ah, I see – you're Vicky, right?"

Angry Bee smirked, one eyebrow still raised in a derisive way. "Yeah? I thought that was obvious."

She glanced away, then back, feeling embarrassed; though she didn't know why. "Well, thanks. It's working now."

He budged her shoulder with his finger, then gestured to her computer. "Any issues, let me know, awright?"

She nodded, her mouth twitching into a quick, closed-mouth smile. She watched his back retreat, then when she was sure his footsteps had faded, she changed her password.

Why did that whole exchange make her feel... What? Incompetent? Yes. Uncomfortable? That too.

***

IceCream365

Savannah typed her password in a second time and the error message popped up again. Her fingers hovered over the keys. If she typed it in wrong one more time, she would be locked out – again.

Always IT problems.

Always on a Monday morning.

Her fingers rested on ASDF and JKL; ready to type, but she didn't press down on any keys yet. It was hard not to second guess herself. Had she used a capital I for icecream? Wait a minute, maybe she had used a capital C for cream. Or was it all lowercase? Was the number 365, or 123?

Oh – my – freakin – gosh. What a *nightmare*.

Ice with a capital, Cream with a capital, three, six and five.

Error message. Locked out.

She swore aloud. Having IT issues every week was making her feel totally incompetent. How could she be trusted with all the accounts she had to manage if she couldn't even handle a simple password change?

Her cheeks burned as she clicked to open a new email on her phone. She had no choice but to see if Vicky was free.

As though reading her mind, her office door swung open and he strode in, wearing his yellow and black Angry Bee tracksuit.

"Er, Vicky? Do you have a moment?"

***

Savannah. Sa-VAH-nah. Sah-VAN-nah.

Yep, that was definitely her. He knew from the light brown highlights. Her hair was pinned in two bunches and with her head tipped to one side, gave her a sort of schoolgirl look in the picture. All coy, like. Cute profile photo.

He clicked 'Add friend' and the box changed to 'Friend request sent'.

Wonder what other photos she had up on her page? All her other profile pictures were set to private. There was nothing on her profile page, other than some songs and TV shows she had liked. Wouldn't be long til he could have a browse through them all.

***

Was that a friend request from Vicky?

Savannah stared at her phone. Why on earth would he send her a friend request after a few IT problems. They hardly knew each other. She blinked a few times, forcing her mind to work. If she deleted the friend request, it would make things awkward in the office. On the other hand, she only accepted friend requests from friends and family who she knew well, so she definitely didn't intend to accept it.

What was best? Best to ignore it for now. She could pretend she hadn't seen it. That was the most practical course of action to take to make work as smooth as possible. Especially like needing to rely on Vicky so much for her computer issues.

Like now.

This time, her password was working and nothing was unplugged at the back – at least as far as she could see. No, this time it was only the keyboard that seemed to be frozen. So frustrating.

She logged into her work emails on her phone and clicked to start a new message to Vicky.

Hi Vicky,

Just having an issue with my keyboard this morning. It seems to be frozen. When you get a moment, could you come and have a look please?

Thanks,

Savannah

A few seconds later, a response popped up. That quick, huh? Vicky must have been checking his work emails on his phone like her. Either that or sitting at his computer. Handy if he was, since his office was on the other side of hers. She read the response.

Hey, no problem. Be there soon, always happy to help u. also saw today that u have a new biker jacket really suits u along with ur signature shoes! Quite a signature look!

Vicky :)

Was she wearing a new jacket? Savannah turned and glanced over her shoulder at the black biker jacket on the back of her chair. It wasn't new; she'd had it for years, but it was the first time she had worn it to work. After so many frogs lately, she had finally swiped right on a prospective prince, and so the jacket was more suited to a dinner date straight after the nine to five than her usual long, wool trench coat.

What an odd thing for Vicky, a colleague, to say, though. When had he seen her? She hadn't seen him; not that morning anyway.

Savannah looked down at her stilettos. She always wore her camel-coloured stilettos. They were comfortable and practical and could also be dressed up, or down, depending on whether she had a date after work like that night, or not.

Once again, Angry Bee had put her in an awkward situation; what should she reply? Best to give a vague thanks for his forthcoming help with her ongoing IT issues and ignore the rest.

Hi Vicky,

Oh, thank you! S :)

It felt strange to be using exclamation marks and smiley faces in a work email – she was always used to being so professional – but she simply wanted to emulate his tone, which had been casual. Her gut feeling told her to keep Vicky *sweet*, particularly since she had to rely on him so much. She would simply avoid the other awkward stuff. Like *funny* comments and friend requests.

No sooner than the thoughts had crossed her mind, another response from Angry Bee popped up on her phone.

Ur welcome! Always look fwd to helping u on Mondays when ur wearing the sandy shoes. The jacket-shoes combo is a good look and suits ur highlights too. U suit the high heeled look most def! :)

Savannah clapped her hand over her mouth.

So, he had taken the 'thank you' as a response to only his comments on her clothing, and not her gratitude over his IT support.

There was no way she could wait for him to come and fix her computer after such comments. No. She had to go and see her line manager right away. She needed advice.

***

Derek. What a dickhead for a boss. Derek the dickhead. Had a good ring to it. That would be his new name.

Derek the Dickhead siding with someone else, not him.

Derek the Dickhead said, 'Do you know what this is about?' and went on to say that there was a complaint about inappropriate comments made by him to another employee in an email.

As if he didn't know who the snitch was.

As if his comments had even been inappropriate. Snitch-bitch couldn't take a fucking compliment.

Derek the Dickhead had asked him if he knew who might have reported such a complaint.

Like, what else could he say to that except – nothing. Say nothing, just shrug.

S for Savannah.

S for snitch.

S for snake.

A snake in the fucking grass.

"Considering you've only been working here for a month," Derek the Dickhead had droned on.

Yeah, and what? Been nice to everybody in a month. Helped their IT problems in a month. Helped Savannah the Snake more than everyone else in a month.

"Stick to acceptable etiquette when dealing with women in the workplace and only talk about work-related issues. No compliments. End of. Even if you mean something as a compliment, it can be misconstrued by the fairer sex."

How fucking condescending was that? What the fuck would Derek the Dickhead know about women anyway? Fat bastard. Bet his fucking wife was as fat as a fucking hippo.

And the fat bastard hadn't even stopped there. Had the nerve to mention Carly. Asked, "You do have a fiancée, don't you?"

Sure. Who wouldn't have grinned at that point? Maid in the living room, chef in the kitchen, whore in the bedroom, like.

"In that case, do yourself a favour and save your compliments for your missus."

Derek the Dickhead. Bet he didn't compliment the old slag he kept locked up at home.

Savannah. S for Savannah, S for Snitch. S for Snake. How could she betray him like that? The bitch would have to pay. He had only ever been nice. Kindness was free. Malice came with a cost.

***

Monday mornings came around too fast. Savannah was tense as she walked along the corridor towards her office. Somehow it felt like a death march. That made sense, given she had reported Vicky the previous Friday afternoon and hadn't yet seen him after the fact.

She pushed the door of her office open and turned on all the lights. The first thing she did was check her computer; nothing unplugged. Could the unplugged wires, and all the password issues she'd had have been anything to do with Vicky?

Surely not. Why would he have done such a thing?

To have a chance to talk to her. The small voice, in the back of her mind, piped up and she forced her thoughts away to distract herself. Best to look at her positive affirmations and think good thoughts.

Savannah's breath caught in her throat. Instead of: *Stay positive and make it happen; Happiness starts with a smile; Make a change starting with your mindset* and *Live in the moment,* her affirmations had been replaced by different mantras written in a similar font and style to the ones she had tacked onto the walls. Her eyes skidded over: *Even broken crayons still colour; keep smiling, it's not worth the jail time; sarcasm is like punching people in the face with words* and *I choose to be happy for it drives people crazy.*

What the actual–?

Before she had a chance to think, her office door slammed open. Vicky stormed through in a whirlwind of cold air, glowering at her. No greeting, nothing. Savannah's heart leapt into her throat. The angry energy he radiated felt like knives pricking her skin with a thousand acupuncture needles.

She wanted to ask him why he had replaced her posters?

Why so secretive about it?

Why the strange comments?

Instead she fled. Coat still on, computer still off, lights not yet on; out of her office.

***

How could she do that? How could she be so callous?

After all their chats. How he'd bonded with Savannah over her computer problems. She'd been so cute, playing coy, peering up at him, all helpless, like. Leading him on.

Some friend. Just another bitch, like the rest. The doctor said he'd needed at least a week off, on stress leave. The look on Derek the Dickhead's face when he'd told his bastard boss. So fucking funny how both Derek the Dickhead's eyebrows nearly hit the roof at the same time.

Savannah was just another bitch, like all women. Fine; if that was how the slut wanted to play things, then he would have some fun too. If she wanted to betray their friendship, then he would take things to the next level.

He looked at the time in the bottom right corner of his screen. An hour to go and then he'd be free for the next week, sitting at home, living it up with Carly, getting her to bring him breakfast in bed. But for now, on last thing to do–

He had created the account a while back, maybe six months back, intending it for Carly – as 'insurance' just in case she ever decided to ditch him. Turned out Carly was safe, like. She would never betray him. She was different. But not this one. This one deserved to have the account in her name.

He logged in to the profile and hit the 'edit' button.

***

What a relaxing weekend she'd had. For once, online dating had paid off as her recent dinner dates with Marcus had been lovely. With his floppy brown hair and green eyes, he looked every part of his Irish ancestry, even though he'd been born and raised in Maida Vale. The previous week at work had ended on a high note, with her line manager, Liselle, informing her that Vicky had been spoken to about his behaviour and was going to be taking some time off to reflect on how to conduct himself around women in the workplace. For once in the past month, Savannah was feeling optimistic about coming into work on a Monday morning.

Speaking of Liselle... Savannah opened her office door to find her boss sitting at her desk. Liselle's body language was closed off; her arms folded across her chest and her right leg strapped over her leg.

"Hi Liselle. How are you? Did you have a nice weekend?" Savannah took off her coat and hooked it on the peg on the back of her office door.

"Savannah, we had an anonymous report about a public profile that has come to our attention. As you know, we're a relatively young Software company. As a Junior Benefits consultant, you're one of our first customer facing people, and we rely on your – our – reputation to deliver first class results and grow our profile in a competitive market–"

Gosh, Liselle could be annoying. Why couldn't her boss get to the freaking point already, instead of giving her the mandatory, company rehearsed speech.

Liselle sighed. "It's better if I show you."

Savannah was half-expecting Liselle to sign in on her computer, but instead, her boss placed her own iPad on its stand and turned it to show her.

An email addressed to Liselle showed on the screen. Savannah skimmed the text:

Dear Liselle,

Please see the following public profile, that involves an employee and violates the ethos of this company.

Yours

Anon.

Savannah looked at the link. The website address showed that it was from a pornographic website. After the dot com, a string of numbers suggested that the link showed an individual profile.

She frowned. "What's this?"

"I had to open it on my personal iPad as the company computers have thankfully blocked such filth." Liselle clicked on the link.

In the thumbnail profile, she saw a picture of herself, her hair in two bunches. It was her profile picture, that she used on several of her online accounts. Underneath, she saw thumbnail photos that had been uploaded. Savannah's jaw dropped. All of the images displayed her either scantily clad or naked. In some pictures, she wore only a fluffy, pink thong. In others, she had tasselled nipple covers. Some showed real penises, ejaculating fluid all over her tanned, toned midriff. In one, she was on her knees, her legs splayed, holding a large, black dildo underneath peephole underwear that showed her shaved genitals.

Except the pictures weren't her.

"You can't possibly think that this is me, that I would do something like that?" Savannah gasped.

Liselle hugged her folded arms higher across her chest, in a defensive pose. "What am I supposed to think? It's your face, isn't it?"

"Yeah, photoshopped onto someone else's body – clearly." Savannah pointed at the screen. "Look at the bodies compared to my face. The skin tone doesn't quite match, does it. Those aren't even my breasts!"

Liselle studied the pictures where Savannah indicated, her lip curled in disgust.

Savannah looked back to the email screen and her hand flew to her mouth. Although addressed to Liselle, the email had been copied to 'All staff'.

"You know what I think? I think Vicky did this. He must have been upset that I reported him last week and did this as a revenge thing," Savannah continued.

Her boss shook her head slowly. "I thought that too, but the account was created six months ago. He wasn't even working for us half a year ago. Derek said he only started last month."

"Around the time I started to have IT problems every week." Savannah clucked her tongue in outrage. "He's an IT support technician, I'm sure he would know how to make a new account seem like it was created longer ago."

She clicked on one of the thumbnail photos to enlarge it, then right clicked to get the information up about it. The jpeg had been uploaded two days before, on Saturday afternoon. She clicked on another, and another. "See what I mean? All these photos were uploaded over the weekend. He's not very smart, this bloke. I'm sure it was him, as revenge porn. I don't know whose body he used, but the face is mine, taken from all of my different social media accounts."

Liselle frowned. "Why don't you use the same profile picture for all of your accounts?"

"Why not? I use all of my socials for different things. Me in a different style reflects my tone on all of those accounts." Savannah shrugged.

Liselle's face relaxed and she finally dropped the folded arms. "Well, whatever is going on is a problem. I'll get Derek to look into it for us. We need the account removed as soon as possible, before it starts appearing on searches. We can't have our reputation damaged over this. I'd suggest using an Avatar on your social media profiles in the interim, and maybe upload a new photo on business accounts wearing business attire to make it more difficult for anyone to use your face in a similar way again."

Liselle closed the iPad and left Savannah's office. Savannah sat down on her chair, not sure what to think, or how to feel.

***

"We think that perhaps our firm isn't the right fit for you. We would be happy to provide you with a satisfactory reference in your journey to finding another position more suited to your skills."

How insulting. How fucking rude. He was effectively being fired. That was a GENTLE push before a BIG push. A 'we're telling you casually in person before we put it in writing and sack your ass' kind of message.

He fumed. He kicked the glass front door open with one foot, his hands full with a cardboard box carrying his mug, his framed picture with Carly in Paris, his Batman calendar and some stationery; as well as five spare company iPads. He smirked to himself. A bit of something for his trouble.

He dumped the box on the passenger seat, started the ignition, but sat for a moment, the vibration of the engine kicking his brain into gear. What now? He couldn't go back to his old job because of a bitch there who'd taken something the wrong way. What was it with fucking women? Too much fucking PMS, or some other shit like that. Whatever. They were all the same. That's why he needed insurance; the account he had created as a way to get back at the wrong ones.

Better be careful next time, though. Bit stupid of him, being an IT bloke and all, to not have realised the I.P. address could be traced back to him. Very stupid. Must have been that bitch, Savannah, ratting him out, insisting they did an investigation.

Savannah; what a coincidence.

She walked out of the building, busy texting, eyes on the phone and not on her whereabouts. Still looking good in those sand-coloured high heeled shoes, her curvy ass showing in those tight leggings.

Whatever. Bitch was the same as all the rest. Except for Carly. Carly didn't know what had happened. Like last time, he'd tell her he didn't like the job, needed to find something else.

Savannah walked across the car park, in his direct line of sight. No time for thought. He stepped on the accelerator. Fast, too fast. She turned, and her eyes became round and her mouth became a perfect circle of surprise to match, lit up in the headlights of his car.

A thud. Black biker jacket, sand-coloured shoes, up over the bonnet of his car. She landed, face down, her head to the left side, hair spread in all directions.

Bitches.

Snitches.

Snitches got stitches.

***

What was that? A car. Bright lights. Pain. Darkness.

And light. Bright light.

And beeps. But not from her.

She sat up. She was in a hospital bed. Where? How? For how long?

"Mum?"

"Savannah. You're awake."

Savannah tried to sit, but felt a stinging pain, and stopped. "Ouch. What happened. How did I get here?"

"You were knocked down in a hit and run." Her mum sounded weary. Looked weary too, her eyes tired and puffy.

"How long have I been here?"

"A month. You had a lot of swelling in your head, so they put you in an induced coma."

Savannah reached up, on instinct, and let her fingers scuttle over the top of her head. There were stitches on the crown, the hair stubby where it was starting to grow back.

She was wearing a neck brace and seated upright on her mattress. "I don't remember what happened."

"We were told it was a colleague of yours who got sacked for harassing you. Honey, why didn't you tell your Dad and I that you had a stalker?"

Wait; it was all coming back. On the same day that Liselle had shown her the fake porn site account that Vicky had made, she had been leaving work, when suddenly she had heard an engine rev up and bright headlights getting closer.

"Angry Bee," said Savannah. "Where is he? Vicky. Is he out on bail?"

"The police are investigating. So far he denies doing it on purpose. He said it was dark, and he didn't see you crossing out in front of him all of a sudden."

"Surely nobody believes that after the fake profile he made of me," Savannah added.

The cheek of that creepy IT guy; what gall he had to lie to the police!

"He won't admit to anything."

Savannah's eyes slipped past her mum to the get-well cards on the hospital bedside table. Aside from the usual designs of balloons and flower prints, one stood out as different. It was a picture of a turtle on its back, wearing sandy coloured shoes. The caption said, 'Hope you're back on your feet soon'. She lifted the card and opened it.

A handwritten note read, 'Get well soon'.

The long, spiky handwriting leaned backwards towards the left. Who wrote like that in an extreme slant? Chicken scratch handwriting.

She flipped the card over. *Signature Style* cards.

She looked again at the company.

Signature.

Signature shoes. Vicky's words, complimenting her in an email. A turtle on its back wearing sandy coloured shoes, like her stilettos.

Vicky. Could it be? Could he be stalking her, gloating over her misfortune?

Shoes and jacket. Signature shoes. A signature look.

Maybe. Was it Angry Bee, boasting about the fact that he had caused her accident; that he had control over how she now lay, immobile, in a hospital bed. A turtle flailing on its back, its 'signature shoes wavering in the air.

A signature look.

Four

The Breadcrumb Trail

Jack lifted the last laundry bag out of the moving van and huffed as he hauled it into his new house. A woman was watching him over the hedge that divided their properties. She wore neatly pressed trousers with a crease down the front and a heavy knitted jumper with a high neckline. She looked to be in her early forties, but her clothing and short, curly brown hair reminded him of his septuagenarian grandmother's style. She carried a coffee mug in one hand.

"Good day to you." The woman smiled widely.

"And to you."

Jack approached the hedge and extended his hand towards her. The woman offered her fingertips in a limp handshake. Her skin felt tepid and clammy; probably because she was standing outside in the chilly autumn weather. A notion to wipe his hand on his trousers crossed his mind, but he refrained, as that would have been rude.

"I'm Hazel," she said.

"Jack," he responded.

"I was wondering who was going to move in, ever since I saw the for-sale sign go down a couple of months ago. You're rather young for a homeowner, aren't you? Most first-time buyers are in their thirties, I thought, what with the state of the economy. You don't look a day over twenty-one."

How did she manage to keep smiling the whole time she spoke? Her eyes crinkled, almost shut, because she smiled so widely.

"Twenty-four, actually."

Not that such information was any of her business; so why did he feel the need to clarify? No point telling her that his parents had helped him to get onto the property ladder, or that he was nervous as a city boy starting his new accounting job in a rural village. Even though she was a new neighbour, she was still a stranger.

"Well, if you ever need anything – a cup of sugar, or even just a chat, then pop on over and knock on my door. I'm usually home."

Hazel didn't wait for his response. Still smiling, she turned and shuffled back inside her house, without so much as a backward glance. Did that make his response an obligation by default? So what if it did; she was being friendly and in any case, it was good to have a neighbour willing to help. He had lived in Ealing for two years, and hadn't met any of his neighbours during that time. Everyone had remained strangers, even though he had heard their laughter, fights, and even lovemaking through the paper-thin walls in the block of flats. He had come to know them as close as friends, without even being acquainted, and in the hallways, lifts or communal areas, they hadn't even made eye contact, never mind exchanged a few friendly words. Wasn't it better to get to know a neighbour properly?

Yes. Jack was thankful that Hazel had come out of her house to welcome him to the neighbourhood.

***

Ding dong.

That couldn't be his delivery, could it? The new bookshelf wasn't due until Thursday; although, if it was, it would be a good time for it. Jack didn't start his new job for a few more days yet, so he would have time to get it unpacked and maybe start assembling it, rather than having to wait until the weekend. As he headed towards the front door, he glanced at the boxes of books blocking the hallway beside the stairs. The sooner he got them unpacked and organised, the better.

A female outline behind the opaque glass panel in the door hinted at grey hair and a grey jumper; it couldn't be anyone other than his new neighbour, Hazel.

He opened the door. She stood grinning, her eyes crinkled, as she held a plate of autumn-leaf shaped biscuits towards him.

"Hello Jack. I hope I'm getting you at a good time. I made you these cookies. They're gluten free, just to be sure you can eat them, as I didn't think to ask yesterday."

"Thanks Hazel. I'm very fortunate that I can eat anything, but it's still very thoughtful of you." He took the plate from her. Her eyes travelled from the plate to the nearest box of books behind him. The flaps were open as he had rummaged for a bedtime read the evening before. Showing on top of the pile was a novel that his ex, Ariana, had bought for him. The cover of *Guilty Pleasures* showed a shapely woman draping a white satin sheet in front of her naked body, her ample cleavage peeking above it. One leg jutted in front of the sheet, clad in a black, lacy stocking enhancing the curve of her nude hip. The only part of her face that showed on the cover was her mouth, the full, red lips parted in a sexy pout. Glossy auburn hair cascaded over one shoulder. It had been a Valentine's Day present, the sole erotic book he owned. Hazel's eyes lingered on the cover.

Jack extended his right knee to the side, pressing the cardboard flap down to conceal the cover, but it was too late. Her fixed smile stretched even wider than before, and her eyes seemed to sparkle with the sliver of intimate knowledge she had gleaned from him.

"I'll give you your plate now, if you like," he said, hoping to cover the awkwardness. "Give me a moment to transfer these over."

"No need," she replied. "You can drop it over to me later."

With that, she turned and left, offering a hint of a smile over her shoulder, and leaving him with a niggling sense of embarrassment.

***

Jack stood back and admired his handiwork. The bookcase had taken a lot more elbow grease than the instructions indicated it would. Instead of slotting into place easily, the pegs for the shelves had needed to be hammered into the pre-cut holes and he'd even needed to use his body weight at one point to force one into place.

At least it was finished; thank goodness as he would now have a free weekend. Sweat pooled under his armpits and dotted his chest; he stood up and pulled off his t-shirt, tossing it onto the floor beside the empty bookshelf packaging.

Movement outside registered in the corner of his eye. Jack glanced out at his garden and then across at the neighbouring one. Was it his imagination, or had someone been watching him, before darting under the cover of the bushes once he looked outside?

He stared more closely. Yes, he was positive that he could see a pair of brown loafers among the leaves, not quite hidden by the sparse grass. Interesting. Jack stooped and grabbed his sweaty t-shirt, then pulled it back on. He approached the window to look more clearly.

There were no shoes. Nobody was hiding behind the bushes.

He hadn't imagined it; Hazel had been watching him from her garden.

Jack shrugged it off. If she'd had a glimpse of his bare chest, it wasn't the worst thing in the world to happen. Maybe he'd been standing too close to the living room window. If anything, it was a reminder to be more aware of what people could see when looking into his house.

One by one, he organised his books, using different shelves for fiction and non-fiction. It was a good feeling to see the cardboard boxes gradually emptying. He made sure to set *Guilty Pleasures* aside though; that one was destined for the built-in closet in his bedroom. Not the photo though; Ariana had enclosed a snapshot of them together in happier times, which he left on his bedside table. Did he still have feelings for his ex? Maybe so. She had dumped him after all, not the other way around.

After he'd finished organising the bookshelf, Jack put on a load of laundry. He carried the basket through to the garden, bright with autumn sunshine, and starting hanging the clothes up on the line.

"Hello again, neighbour."

Jack turned to see Hazel peering over the five-foot high wooden fence.

"Oh, hi Hazel," he said.

"It's lovely weather for the laundry, isn't it?"

"I guess so. It would be better if the wind picked up too, to dry it in half the time."

"I see you're a fan of T&A. I'm quite partial to supermarket clothing myself, mind you. Seems to be good quality fabric."

T&A? Didn't she mean P&A, the chain-store brand of clothing, not T&A? Didn't that mean 'tits' and 'ass'? Jack looked down at the clothes in his laundry basket, and the ones on the line. Regardless of the implication, she had a good eye, if she could tell the brand just from looking at the fabric. None of the labels were obvious.

"Oh, while you're here, let me get your plate for you. Thanks again for the cookies, by the way. They were delicious." He brought the plate out to her and passed it over the fence.

"Not a problem, my dear. I love baking, so any time you want a sweet treat, I can make you a batch."

She turned towards her house with a small wave goodbye. He watched her greying head bob alongside the fence until she climbed the three steps leading towards her kitchen door. As she walked inside her house, he saw that she wore light brown loafers.

He hadn't imagined it after all; she had seen him topless through his living room window.

Jack stooped and grabbed the empty laundry basket, before going back in his house. He dumped it in the kitchen and walked through to the hallway, past the full-length mirror near the door. The t-shirt that he had chosen, after he had stripped off the sweaty one, was tight-fitting and rode high, so that he could see the elastic waistband of his boxers above the top of his jeans. Out of curiosity, he stretched his arms up, in the same manner he might when he pinned laundry onto the washing line.

His reflection showed his exposed stomach, along with the waistband of his boxers, displaying the letters P&A.

Hazel had been reading the label of his boxers.

Hmm. That was a bit odd, was it not? He thought about the situation. It probably wasn't so odd for someone to take a quick glance at someone's underwear, if such things were on display. But to make a comment on such things to a person you hardly knew was a tad strange.

Maybe she found him attractive. He wasn't too bad looking, if he was honest. He didn't work out, though was naturally slim, and his ears stuck out a bit much. But besides that, he was a 'tall dark and handsome' type; although the handsome part was more like a 'bit of alright'. If Hazel found him attractive, it was a harmless thing. She was an older woman. There was nothing wrong with an ego boost, especially after Ariana had dumped him so callously after they got back from their holiday in Turkey.

So be it. He couldn't blame Hazel. Nothing but innocent fun.

***

"Hello Jack. Will you be attending the autumn fair today?"

Jack jumped. Hazel stood behind him in the corner shop queue, smiling the same as always. She was wearing a red roll-neck jumper and black corduroy leggings. The change in both colour and form-fitting style made a stark difference from how she had previously dressed.

"I wasn't aware of any autumn fair. Where will that be then?"

"It's in the village square, opposite the community centre. I can stop by your door, and we can go together, if you like?"

"That's very kind of you. What time does it start?"

"I'll pick you up at two o'clock, shall I?"

"Sounds perfect." Jack turned his attention back to the till, aware that Hazel's eyes were scouring his small bundle of groceries; she had stepped to one side to see what he was buying. He smirked to himself. Village folks were probably bored from time to time and relished having new faces to bring fresh excitement to the place. Nonetheless, he was glad his shopping list had only been inoffensive items: teabags; milk; a lighter; batteries and a chocolate bar. He thanked the cashier and took the bag she handed him, his mind on what to do with the afternoon.

An afternoon which disappeared, as quickly as it arrived. He whittled away the hours enjoying autumn leaves on the trees in the churchyard and noticing hundreds of starlings sitting on the boom of a crane that stretched across the main road, from a construction site in the grounds of the primary school. He wasn't the best photographer but snapped a few pictures; he could play around with the contrast and settings later. Simple pleasures.

Hazel's outline appeared behind the glass panel of his front door at two o'clock on the dot. *Punctual.*

"Ready for the fair?"

Jack looked down at an envelope in his hand, that she held out to him. "What's this?"

"A little something to welcome you to the town," she said with a smile.

He ripped the envelope open. Inside was a handmade card. A row of small birds sat on an autumnal tree, the leaves illustrated in reds, yellows and browns to reflect the weather. The picture was raised, not quite pop-up, but set higher than the card itself. He flipped it open.

Dear Jack. With warmest wishes, your new neighbour, Hazel.

Odd. Getting a welcome card wasn't strange in itself; so what was bothering him?

He set the card on top of the electricity box in his hallway, and grabbed his coat off the hook by the door on his way out. Hazel led the way down his garden path, and they stepped out onto the street.

"You don't mind if I hold onto your arm, do you? Sometimes I find that the autumn leaves can be slippery and I lose my balance," said Hazel.

Jack looked along the street. There were a few leaves gathered by the kerb, but the ground was dry; definitely no potential slip hazards. Before he had a chance to reply, she hooked her arm through the crook of his elbow, her woollen-gloved hand dangling off his arm. Oh well. If he was honest, he wasn't the most tactile of people, but he would have felt bad to refuse; besides the fact it would be awkward.

"Are you a student then, Jack?" she asked.

"No, I graduated a few years ago. I'm starting a new job at a company near here, and it's a great location. I like being able to walk to work."

"Oh? What company?"

Jack paused. "Just an accountancy firm."

"What about your parents? Are they going to be moving in with you too?"

He bristled. Why so many questions? Were they normal 'getting to know you' questions? He couldn't say; he personally liked to keep to himself and not ask anyone too much about themselves, too soon. People opened up if you gave them time. Plus, her questions made him feel *guarded*, though he couldn't put his finger on why.

"No, I'm living by myself."

She beamed, widely. "How charming. In that case, you can be my bosum companion, neighbour."

What an old-fashioned thing to say. Jack chuckled to himself, turning his head so she wouldn't see.

Hazel led the way, steering Jack by their linked arms and soon he saw a series of stalls set up in rows under a large, white tarpaulin. The autumn fair looked to be an intimate affair with everyone mingling and chatting with familiarity; much as he had expected in a small locale. As they approached, a middle-aged woman wearing a white body warmer and spectacles turned her attention away from her cakes to greet them with a smile.

"Hello, Hazel. Glad to see you up and about again after your fall." She turned to Jack and a devious twinkle formed in her eyes. "And who is this?"

"This is Jack. Jack, this is Izzy."

Izzy tipped her chin downwards, peering over the top of her glasses. "A young man, I see."

Hazel pressed her lips together in a knowing smile, before responding. "Yes, well, fresh faces in our village are very welcome, wouldn't you say?"

"You wouldn't be a day over twenty-four, would you, Jack?" said Izzy, still watching over the top of her glasses.

"Good guess. I'm exactly that," he said, without mirth.

"And if you switch those numbers, you'll have the age of your fabulous tour guide. A perfect match, then?" Izzy continued.

So, Hazel was forty-two. He had reckoned as much.

"Yes, well don't let us keep your customers away, Izzy, although it doesn't seem there are too many around at the moment anyway," said Hazel. "I wouldn't want you to have all your cakes – and eat them too, so to speak."

The women laughed, but it seemed to be forced merriment. Maybe Hazel and Izzy were frenemies. Whatever the issue, was none of his business.

Jack felt himself steered onwards to the next stall. He slid a sideways glance at Hazel. She had a quietly satisfied smile on her face. He looked back at Izzy and caught her smiling at his ass, before she let her eyes travel up his body to meet his gaze, and gave him a wink.

A young man, I see. Yes, he was young, being only twenty-four. There was something in the way she said it that struck him. Sort of, to imply that there was a romantic liaison between him and Hazel. Is that what she meant? Also, what did it matter if he was twenty-four, and Hazel forty-two? There was nothing to stop neighbours of any age associating with each other; nothing taboo about that.

Hazel squeezed his arm. "Don't mind Izzy. She's a flirt at the best of times."

He shrugged his shoulder; of the arm she had hooked hers through. "It's fine. I thought she seemed nice."

Hazel's smile faded, and she fluttered her eyelashes, as though batting away his response. "We go way back. We went to school together. She left the village for a while, then came back, whereas I never left here at all."

"Well then, it's good for me to have an experienced tour-guide. Someone who knows this village like the back of their hand." He smiled at Hazel.

Hazel grinned back, and any tension that had been in her expression from Izzy melted away.

***

The thing about living in a village was the silence. Silence punctuated by occasional birdsong. He had been used to the hustle and bustle of London, even in a comparatively quiet suburb such as Ealing, but now the lack of noise of village life was obvious. More than obvious; stark.

So stark, that the rustle of paper on wood travelled upstairs and reached him in bed.

Jack peeled the duvet back and swung his legs out of bed. He padded downstairs in his boxers and saw a small, rectangular package that lay on the doormat.

Post on a Sunday? He picked it up. No address label, or any writing at all. Odd. He turned the package over in his hands, then flipped it back. The neatly folded ends had been sticky-taped with a line at either side. Curious.

Jack unlocked the door and popped his head outside, looking to the left, then right. Nobody was about. Only signs of life, in fact, were a few birds tweeting their morning greeting in a tree in Hazel's garden.

He swung the door shut and brought the package through to the kitchen to set on the counter. It wasn't important. First things first; he was thirsty. There was a jug of orange juice in the fridge that would do the job.

Jack eyed the package while he sipped. It was the size and weight of a book. Who had pushed a book through his letterbox?

He scratched his head and set down his glass of juice to rip open the package.

Guilty Pleasures: Love-cuffed liaisons.

What on earth? Jack chuckled out loud, into the silence of the room. Who had sent him a dirty book?

Ariana. His mind drifted to an image of his admittedly beautiful ex, with the glossy, black coils that framed her face, her long, slim, legs and coffee-coloured skin. Their six-month relationship had fizzled before it ever got started; in retrospect, her Valentine's gift of 'Guilty Pleasures' had been a hint to spice up the chemistry between them. She was extroverted and charismatic, a complete opposite of his quiet introversion. Why on earth would his vivacious ex send him a sequel to an erotic novel that had failed to save their doomed romance the previous year?

The answer was, she hadn't. Who had, then?

It couldn't be Hazel, could it? He recalled how she had looked at the titles among his open box of books in the hallway. Fair enough, Guilty Pleasures had been on top; but that didn't mean she had noticed that title in particular, did it?

Should he ask her? What if he was wrong; it was an awkward thing to bring up, considering it was an erotic title. If it had been a guide to birdwatching, maybe, or a history book about the local area, perhaps. If he brought it up, and was wrong, it would be a huge point of embarrassment.

He eyed the book with suspicion as he made himself a herb omelette with fried tomatoes for breakfast, then went through to the living room to eat his meal and see what was on the box. The faux leather sofa felt good against his bare back. He made a mental note to turn down the heating when he next got up. There were pros and cons to living alone: pros like being able to eat breakfast in nothing but his boxers, and cons like having no one there to turn down the heating – or do anything else for that matter – for him. If his mum was there right now, she would've told him to put on a t-shirt. But she also would have made him a cup of tea to go with his omelette.

"Hello? Jack?"

The words were followed by two quiet raps. Jack sprung out of the soft cushions on his sofa, nearly sending his omelette flying to the floor. Hazel stood in the open living room doorway.

"Sorry, I didn't mean to startle you," she said, softly.

"Hazel! How did you get in?"

"I knocked, but there was no answer, so I tried the handle and it was open." An apologetic smile was on her face, but it had limits; her eyes travelled down to Jack's bare chest and abdomen and a hint of approval washed any tacit apology away.

He set his plate down on the sofa and snatched the patchwork blanket that he had folded and left on one armrest. It had been a gift from his grandmother – and he was grateful for it, now more than ever. He slung it over his shoulders and held it in place like a cloak with one hand. Thank goodness he had chosen to wear his loose-fit cotton boxers, rather than the tight-fitting sports style ones that he saved for dates. Her eyes lingered on his body, travelling lower, and lower, until they rested on his crotch for a second too long, then jumped to meet his. A knowing smile played on her face.

"I was going to ask if you wanted a brownie. I made some yesterday evening."

His cheeks burned. "Erm, no. That's alright. I don't actually have much of a sweet tooth, really."

"So I see. You're very slim. If anything, you could do with some fattening up."

Another excuse to ogle his half-naked body, it seemed. Jack pulled more of the patchwork blanket over his front half, hiding behind the woollen barricade that kept her greedy eyes off him.

Since things were now quite awkward between them anyway, he figured he might as well find out more about the book. That way he could rule Hazel – or his ex – out of the picture, at the very least.

"While you're here, I wonder if I could ask a quick question. Someone pushed a brown package through my letterbox this morning. It wouldn't have been you by any chance, would it?"

"Oh?" she said, without any indication of surprise. "What sort of package?"

"A book, actually. There was no address on it, or any return information, so it I think someone did it by themselves."

Her face showed mild interest. "Well, I suppose they would have had to, wouldn't they? There's no post on a Sunday."

"It wasn't you, then?" He raised an eyebrow.

The corners of her mouth turned upwards, as her interested smile stretched further. "Was it a book you like, at least?"

Quite evasive; he was going to have to work further to get a direct answer from her. "Not especially. I mostly read non-fiction, to be honest."

She pressed her lips together, interest changing to amusement. "That's a pity. Hopefully you'll find some use for it sometime, then."

With that, Hazel turned and left, closing Jack's front door with a soft, but audible click. Still clutching the patchwork blanket around his shoulders, he slipped out into the hallway and turned the key in the lock.

***

There was a definite chill in the air, as November set in and autumn began to pave the way for winter.

Not that it felt that way in his house. His heating bills would be through the roof at this rate. It was hard to manage keeping a whole house warm, compared to his flat in Ealing. Of course, he wouldn't have swapped them for the world. No more having to hear every conversation through thin walls or having people living above with their constant noisy footsteps.

He walked through into the kitchen to turn down the dial on the gas.

No wonder it was so hot. Had he really cranked it up to max? He was pretty sure he had left it switched off overnight as he didn't need the heat; having a high metabolism was to thank for that. In fact, he had left the kitchen window open to get air flow through the house. It was something he never would have done in his ground floor flat in London for safety reasons, but a rural place felt safe enough; not to mention the fact that the kitchen looked out over his back garden, which was enclosed by a five-foot tall fence.

The heater wasn't on a timer, was it? He looked carefully on all sides of it to double-check. Nothing that he could see. The dial had to be hand-turned.

Oh well. He'd been dog-tired the night before, so maybe he had simply forgot turning it up to max. It was an easy mistake to make; a full rotation clockwise to switch it on, and a full rotation anti-clockwise to turn it off. Maybe he would look to getting a more modern, simpler on-off switch instead to stop any confusion. He rotated the dial the full way anti-clockwise and pushed the window by the kitchen sink even wider to enjoy the crisp, late-autumn breeze.

"Hello neighbour!"

Hazel's face peered over the dividing fence between their gardens, and she gave a small, accompanying wave.

Why did she always seem to be around? What work did she even do? It occurred to him that he didn't actually know what job she did. Must've been something that involved working from home if she was always there.

Speaking of work, he needed to get focused. It was his first day at his new position, and it wouldn't make a good first impression on his new boss to run late. Jack waved back at Hazel, then turned towards the kettle. Coffee, breakfast and preparing a packed lunch were all that he had on his mind right then.

***

Lunch time arrived before Jack knew it. The morning had gone quickly, getting the client files organised and getting up to speed with the firms and individuals that would be his accounts to manage. His new office had a cheery, southern aspect, giving lots of light and such things were important to him. Wellbeing was important, especially in a place he would be spending eight hours a day, for five days a week.

Might be good to pop out for a stretch, even though he had brought his sandwiches with him. He quite liked cold weather, as long as it was sunny.

He took the stairs down two floors to the lobby. The young, red-haired receptionist looked up as he walked towards the door.

"Hi, I'm Elaine," she smiled. "I didn't see you when you came in this morning. How are you enjoying your first day?"

"I'm Jack. Nice to meet you." He reached across and shook her hand. "Settling in well, I think. All my accounts seem fairly self-explanatory."

"That's good." She handed a small, cardboard cake box to him. "Oh, don't forget these."

Jack frowned as he took the box from her. It was tied with a length of twine. He lifted one corner up and peered inside to see six macaroons.

"What's this?" he said, raising an eyebrow.

She searched his face. "I thought you left them here? They had your name on them."

He turned the box around in his hand and saw his name written in the top right corner of one side, but nothing else. "Were they here when I arrived?"

She shook her head. "Someone must have left them for you, if you say it wasn't you. I was in the back office and came out and they were on the counter next to my computer."

Next to her computer, not on the counter. That meant someone had leaned over the counter to place them on her desk, which was lower.

"Nobody was waiting at reception when you came back out?"

Her smile faded, replaced by a contemplative look. "No. I don't think anyone even came in, or there would've been a draught."

Curious. He shrugged. "Maybe it was someone from upstairs then."

Her wide smile returned as she beamed. "How lovely! A welcome present. Everyone is so nice here. That's what I like about it – it's a small, intimate team."

He returned the smile. "Well, do you mind if I pick them up on my way back in? I'm just going out to stretch my legs and I'll be back shortly."

"Not a problem. I'll have them here ready for when you get back."

Jack breezed out into the autumn sunshine. The chill was refreshing, and he found a street bench in a bright spot to eat his sandwiches and admire a wren perched in a tree. As he passed back through reception, on his way up to his office, he made sure to collect the box of macaroons.

"Jack, how are you getting on?" said Colin, his new boss.

"Doing alright so far." He showed the box. "Everyone's so friendly too. I'm not sure who left these, but they're a nice surprise."

Colin looked puzzled. "Maybe Pamela got them earlier."

As if on cue, a brown-haired woman in a skirt-suit walked out of her office, holding a mug that read: 'World's best accountant'.

"That was nice of you, Pam, to get a welcome treat for Jack. Where was mine when I started?"

He playfully swiped at her with a risk analysis sheet he was holding.

Her eyes widened, in mock playfulness. "Wasn't me, though I'll happily take the credit, so long as I get something new in return. How about a company car?"

They laughed. Jack opened the box. "Who would care for a mystery macaroon, then?"

"I wouldn't say no," said Colin.

"Why not?" said Pam.

Jack's eyes dropped once more to his name written in one corner. It wouldn't have been Hazel, would it? She was always offering to bake him some cookies, or whatever he wanted. Why would she have dropped off a box of treats to his work though? More to the point, how would she know *where* he worked? He hadn't explicitly told her.

He made a mental note to ask her later. Asking about baked goods, rather than pornographic books, was a much more palatable subject for a civilised discussion between neighbours.

***

A blast of heat hit Jack as he opened his front door, almost as though the chill from outside had created a vacuum, sucking all the warmth out of his house. He closed and locked the front door, then stripped off his jumper, shirt and tie and hung them on the pegs in the hallway. How on earth did the house retain so much heat? Only the kitchen had a south facing aspect, but even the living room was hot.

Better check to be sure it wasn't the gas heater malfunctioning. He strode into the kitchen and checked the dial. It was switched off, as he had left it that morning.

Strange. Hopefully it wasn't faulty. There was another way to tell; the hot water tap tended to run with lukewarm water if he hadn't used the heating for several hours. He switched it on and let it run for thirty seconds, then put his finger under it. The water was hot.

Great. Just perfect. He would need to call someone from the gas company and get them to send out an engineer to have a look at it. Maybe Hazel would know a reputable company to call; plus it would be a good opportunity to ask about the macaroons.

He pulled his shirt back on but left his jumper and tie hanging on the peg. Hazel's garden was immaculate; further evidence of someone who had all the time in the world to make sure it was perfectly manicured. His neighbour sure was house proud.

Jack stepped up onto her front porch and rang the doorbell. Behind the frosted glass, he saw her outline emerging closer along the hallway.

"Jack! What brings you here? Care to come in for tea and a scone?"

He scratched the back of his neck. "Thanks, that's kind of you, but I'm actually just home from work. I don't want to bother you, but I'm having trouble with my gas boiler and wondered if you might know a good company I could call to send out an engineer?"

Hazel jerked her head, indicating for him to come inside. "I know just the person. Come on in, while I find Stan's number."

He followed her inside, noting how their houses mirrored each other; they had the same design but had been flipped, so that her living room lay on the left, whereas his was on the right, and her stairs leading upwards was against the right side. Like her clothing, Hazel's house gave the impression of a woman much older than forty-two. In fact, it seemed as though it had been decorated by a person in their seventies, or eighties. Two four by four feet canvases, dominating opposite walls, showed nightmarish, abstract paintings of young, dark-haired men; both men looked back over their shoulders, with deer-in-headlights expressions, as though caught unaware. They had been painted in wide, thick lines of acrylic paint as though the paint had been smeared in anger and were semi-dressed; one with only a towel around his waist and the other sun-lounging in tight-fitting shorts. The images were unpleasant; very, unsettling. Other than the paintings, there was an old-fashioned wooden piano in the living room, and a beige rug with garish black swirls all over it. A long, sausage-shaped draught excluder with a dog's face was placed beside the open door and a number of ceramic Egyptian cat statues lined the mantel, above an open fireplace. A small, bronze bucket with wooden logs sat in front of the metal grate. Why would Hazel have a gas engineer's number if she used a wood burner?

"I use gas as well," she explained, as though reading his mind. "The logs are just for aesthetic purposes – and a nice smell."

Jack bristled; why did her comment leave him feeling so – so *exposed*? It was just a coincidence. Hazel wasn't psychic. She probably saw where he was looking and guessed what he was thinking, considering he was there to get a gas engineer's number. Perceptive, not psychic. Seemed she was so good at reading people that she could tell what they were thinking, simply by where they happened to look.

He followed her into her kitchen, the delicious smell of baking wafting out as they entered. While she took a sticky note off her fridge, Jack noticed baking trays in a washing basin inside the sink.

"Have you been rustling up more cookies or brownies?"

Hazel gave a pursed lip smile. "Just a red velvet cake for myself."

"Someone very kindly dropped macaroons off at my work today. I was going to ask if it was you, considering you're such a great baker."

A tinge of pink appeared on her cheeks as a smile spread on her face. "You must have liked my cookies a lot then?"

"Better than even my mum's, and she's great at baking too."

The smile faded, as did the blush. "I'm glad they put you in mind of your mum's baking."

Or did her smile fade because she thought the comparison was between her and his mum? He hadn't meant for her to take it that way; she didn't remind him of his mum at all. She was more than a decade younger than his mum, but dressed three decades older.

"Here's the number for Stan. Give him a call and he'll sort out your gas boiler." She gave him the sticky note, her cool, clammy fingers touching his for the briefest of seconds; Jack retracted his hand with a snap, almost dropping the note in the process. Why did her fingers feel like an eel slithering on his hand? He looked down at the note. She had spelt 'Stan' as 'Satan'. He chortled to himself. Helpful and harmless; but not the most competent at spelling. Endearing. Put him in mind of something his mum would do.

He thanked Hazel and walked back to his house, relieved to have some down-time after his first day of work. Was that why he felt tense? He couldn't say. Something was bothering him, but it was hard to put his finger on what it could be.

It wasn't still the issue of the macaroons, was it? So what if an anonymous person had left them; it was a kind gesture. Even if Hazel had left them, it was a present, not anything to make him tense.

So, why did it make him tense? They were just baked goods, nothing worth stressing over. Or was it the fact that she had been evasive, yet again. She hadn't confirmed one way or another whether she had made them or not; a similar response to how she dodged his question about the mystery book being posted through his door. Mystery objects. Benign presents. But left by who, and for what reason?

***

December arrived bringing snow. It was a welcome sight, in Jack's opinion. Even though Stan had been round to fix the gas boiler, only a week passed before the house seemed to be hot all the time again; particularly when he returned from work, which was odd. He had taken to leaving all of the windows open all the time to get as much throughflow as possible. The house was always cool when he woke up as a result, but back to sub-tropical temperatures by early evening.

He stood on the kitchen doorstep in shorts and a t-shirt, admiring the fluffy flakes falling in the back garden. Maybe by the time he got home from work, it would be lying thick enough to build a snowman.

A familiar scraping sound of a draft excluder brushing a doormat signalled Hazel opening her back door. Jack rolled his eyes. Could he not even enjoy a moment of solace to himself?

Guilt prickled him; she was innocent, simply wanting to build a neighbourly relationship. He put a smile on and turned to greet her over the fence.

At first, Jack didn't recognise the woman who came out. Maybe Hazel had a friend round visiting her house? The shoulder-length, black spirals that had been heavily gelled were unfamiliar, and the spray tan she wore was clearly professionally done, but there was no doubt it was Hazel.

Was she wearing a wig? Hazel's short, mousy hair was normally no longer than ear-length. As she approached the fence with a smile, he saw that it wasn't a wig, as he could see her own hair at the roots, dyed black. Hair extensions, then? He didn't know much about women's hair fashions. More pressing was what to say to her. If he didn't compliment the change, it would be obvious as the change was drastic, but on the other hand he didn't feel they were on familiar enough terms to make a comment about her appearance.

"Hello Jack," she said in a sultry drawl. Was he imagining the sultriness to her greeting? No, there was definitely a certain *tone* to her words. Hazel tugged on one coil that bounced on her left shoulder, twisting it around her finger, while biting the right side of her lip. Yes, he was certain. She was flirting with him.

"Hi Hazel." He cleared his throat. "Quite snowy today."

Her smile faltered a notch. "Oh yes, a bit earlier in the season than we were expecting, I suppose."

She pushed out her chest. She was wearing a white roll-neck jumper and a form-fitting tweed skirt that sat a couple of inches above her knees. The change in clothing made for a completely different look too; much younger than the septuagenarian styles she usually sported. In fact, what she wore wouldn't have looked out of place on a woman his age.

Who did she remind him of? There was something familiar in the style she was going for, but he couldn't put his finger on it. He wasn't entirely convinced her new look suited her, but then who was he to judge?

"Well, I for one am glad for the colder snap."

Hazel didn't let him finish his thought; she cocked her head to one side and flashed a coquettish smile. "Why? Has it been too warm for you?"

The warm air swirling around him from his open kitchen doorway illuminated the thought. Was she implying the heat in his house, or the autumn temperature?

Best to clarify. "It has been unseasonably warm until now, I guess. Though I meant in my house. The gas is still playing up."

"Oh, that's a shame." She gave a playful pout. "I could send Stan round again if you like? If you leave me with your key, I could handle things while you're at work."

He was about to say no but paused the thought. Why not? So what if she was being flirtatious; there was no reason she couldn't have harmless fun. It wasn't as though it would lead to an affair between them. She was closer to his mum's age and besides that fact, not his type. She liked to be a helpful neighbour, clearly, and if it made her feel good about herself to help him, then why not?

"That would be awfully kind of you, would you mind?"

"Not at all, neighbour, isn't that what friends are for?"

He smiled. "In that case, how about I slip the key through your letter-box on my way to work?"

She offered a warm, flaccid handshake in return; a very non-flirtatious, platonic thing to do. More curt, and businesslike, in his opinion than someone who considered him a friend. For some reason, it gave him more confidence in her offer; maybe because she was willing to keep a boundary between them; a tacit agreement of sorts.

***

It had been a good day at work, if very busy. Jack collected his key from Hazel, thankful that she hadn't tried to entice him in for baked goods of any kind and was happy to feel a welcoming coolness inside the house. Stan had clearly seen to the issue with the gas. Hopefully this time it would work with no further problems.

What was there for dinner? As healthy as he normally liked to eat, tonight called for a quick and easy ready meal. He pulled a chicken curry out of the freezer, pierced the film on top and stuck it in the microwave. While it was cooking, he poured a large glass of orange juice from the pitcher in the fridge.

He flopped down on the sofa with his curry and juice and switched on the TV. Maybe a good action film, if there was anything on.

A while later, Jack awoke. He must have nodded off. His half-eaten curry lay on his lap; luckily it hadn't spilled. He looked at the time on his phone. Forty-five minutes had passed. *Yikes*, anything longer than a twenty-minute nap would affect his sleep later that night. Was work really so tough? Guess so.

He took another long drink of orange juice, glugging down the half that remained after his dinner. Soon, a heavy sleepiness swept over him, a feeling of deep tiredness that he had not felt since jetlag after a long haul flight to Australia, when he had been backpacking after university. His eyelids shut, and he fought to open them; shut and he forced them open.

A click of the front door opening alerted him and he tried to focus on the sound to keep himself awake.

Hazel walked into his living room. She was wearing a long, chestnut brown fur coat. The black coils of her hair bounced above her shoulders and he could see that her lips were painted red. She wore matching red stiletto shoes, her ankles above them bare.

His eyes swam in and out of focus. Hazel became a blur of black, and red and brown. Who did she remind him of?

Ariana. His beautiful ex.

Not that Hazel was beautiful, or looked remotely like Ariana, but her hair had been styled the same way and colour and her spray-tanned skin resembled his ex's coffee coloured skin tone too. Could that be on purpose? Hazel hadn't seen any pictures of Ariana. It must have been a coincidence.

Hold on a moment. Tucked in the back of the erotic book, Guilty Pleasures, was a photo of Ariana. She had been wearing a tight-fitting white roll neck top and a checkered skirt – exactly the way Hazel had dressed earlier that morning. Could Hazel have taken a sneaky peek in his bedroom, maybe while Stan was fixing the gas boiler?

But what about this fur-coat business? Jack lay slumped on the sofa, looking up at his neighbour, his head lolling from side to side; drifting on a tide of tiredness.

"Hello, friend," said Hazel.

In one swift move, she whipped open her fur coat revealing that she was nude underneath. Her pale, slim body was angular, with jutting hip-bones and thin, parallel thighs. He could see a hint of ribcage between her small, low breasts. Her brown, bushy pubic hair made a large V in the middle of her narrow body.

Hazel shrugged the fur coat off and it fell, parachute-like, onto the wooden floor.

She wasn't going to try and have sex with him, was she? Apart from the fact that he didn't feel aroused by her, he was too tired.

So tired. So sleepy.

His mind swam in and out of consciousness. Maybe this was a dream. Yes, this had to be a dream. His neighbour had a septuagenarian style about her; definitely not anything like a seductress, or a dominatrix.

Hazel dropped onto all fours on the floor. He could see the prominent bones of her spine as she arched her back, tucking her bottom downwards, then curved her body so that her bottom, and head face upwards. Bucking and writhing, bucking and writhing.

Yes. This had to be a dream. So sleepy.

He watched her, his head lolling in the sofa cushions as she began spanking herself with one hand.

"Bad girl. Bad, bad girl."

The slap of skin on skin.

"Tell me I'm bad and I have to do it," she said.

"Bad?" said Jack, his tongue heavy. "Do what?"

More slaps. "Say it. I'm so bad. I'll do it because you want me to."

"Do what?" he slurred.

"You aren't going to make me, are you? I don't want to do it?"

More slaps. Her bottom was becoming pink.

"Don't make me do it," she panted.

Jack tried to raise his heavy head, but it sank further into the cushions with the effort.

Hazel lowered her head to the floor and began licking the floor. Her wide, pink tongue made wet saliva patches on the wood. Her small, pointed breasts dangled and her bony bottom stuck upwards as she dipped low and licked, dipped low and licked.

"Stop that," Jack protested, his voice weak.

Hazel obeyed. She sat on her knees and placed both hands like paws in front of her bare chest, positioning herself towards him with tongue hanging.

"Yes Master. I'll be a good girl."

"Stop saying that."

This dream wasn't a good one. It was an uncomfortable one. A nightmare, if he was honest. After such a bad dream, he was sure he wouldn't be able to look at Hazel in the same way again.

Hazel grabbed his foot, that had been dangling off the sofa. She pulled his sock off and placed his bare foot on her face. From there, she pushed his foot, sending herself sprawling onto her back on top of her fur coat.

"I've been such a bad girl. I'll try to be good."

What kind of sordid imagination was trapped in his subconscious to evoke this kind of degenerate dream? Could he close his eyes, even within a dream?

Yes. Welcome respite from the unwelcome, and disgusting display before him.

A warm wetness on his big toe made him open his eyes. Hazel was sucking on it, her red lips enclosing it.

"Urgh, get off – right – now!"

Jack jerked his foot away and Hazel fell forwards onto her knees. With all his remaining energy spent, his eyelids grew heavy and his chin slumped forward onto his chest.

***

What a banging headache he had. Jack blinked several times, his eyes adjusting to the stream of light flooding in through a gap in the bedroom curtain.

Such a weird – and disturbing – dream. Hazel, with her hair and skin painted up like his ex, Ariana. Hazel cavorting in the nude... and worse. He cringed at the memory of the dream.

Disgusting. How could his brain betray him like that? Seemed he had been letting intruding thoughts about *Guilty Pleasures: Love cuffed liaisons* get inside his mind. Not that he had even read such trashy filth – or ever would.

He got a shower – needed a shower – dressed for work and went downstairs.

What on earth had been in that takeaway dinner he'd eaten? It seemed he was so used to clean eating that a bit of junk had caused him to have nightmares. His granny had told him as a child that rich food before bed would cause strange dreams. Certainly appeared to be the case, since he recalled getting very sleepy soon after he had finished eating.

His plate and orange juice glass were in the sink. He had no recollection of putting them there. In fact, the last thing he remembered was the bizarre dream involving Hazel. Even the memory made him cringe. He would never be able to look his neighbour in the eye again after such a nightmare.

What on earth had happened in between him eating his microwave meal on the sofa, and falling asleep in his bedroom? Several hours were unaccounted for. The memory gap made him feel very discombobulated. He wandered between living room to kitchen, trying to recall the lost few hours between putting his empty plate and glass in the sink. Nothing on the floor, except a few breadcrumbs. Breadcrumbs, or cookie crumbs. Had he eaten dessert? The cookies that Hazel had given him, and the macaroons, had long since been eaten.

He needed to get out. Yes, going out for breakfast would be the perfect antidote to a strange and unsettling previous evening. He felt hungover, yet he hadn't even touched a drop of alcohol.

Odd. So odd.

Had he been overworking lately? Probably, but not likely. He had poured all his energy into his first week at a new job, as anybody might. But it wasn't as though he had stayed behind doing unpaid overtime, or had taken on more work than the accounts he was responsible for. No, he had been hardworking but prudent, leaving work behind the minute the clock hit five thirty.

Jack shut his door and locked up. He closed his eyes and inhaled, letting the chill air sting his nostrils, the crisp coldness a reminder that he was very much awake and that any disturbing dreams were behind him.

"Hello neighbour."

Hazel's cloying voice made him cringe before he even had time to open his eyes. He chased intrusive images of her cavorting on his living room floor out of his mind. Bad thoughts. Unwelcome thoughts. Why did his mind torture him so much?

Hazel wore a tweed jacket and beige corduroy trousers, along with her brown loafers. Instead of long, black hair extensions and fake tan, her hair was short and mousey brown and her complexion pale, as it usually was.

Jack blinked several times and stared at her.

"I hope the rain holds off, I was hoping to do some gardening," she continued.

He continued staring at her, his brain and mouth not connecting.

Was he going mad? Hadn't Hazel, only yesterday, been wearing black hair extensions and fake tan, along with a tighter-fitting set of clothes? Surely her change in appearance had been what triggered the disturbing sexual dream. He hadn't imagined the entire previous day, had he?

"Are you off to work then?" Hazel smiled.

His brain kicked into gear. "Er, um, yeah. Just about to go. Thank goodness it's Friday."

"Have you any nice weekend plans then, Jack?"

He scratched his head. He really felt like he was going crazy. "Uh – no, nothing much. My friends, Sophie and Aman, are coming up from London, that's all. We might just have a movie night."

"That'll be nice. I'm sure you could do with a few youngsters like yourself around. Village life can get a bit dull."

Jack opened and closed his jaw a couple of times. "Well, I'd better go, or I'll be late. I'll maybe see you around."

She lifted up a trowel and waggled it. "I'll probably still be gardening when you finish work," she laughed.

Who did gardening in December? Hazel sure was eccentric.

He forced a polite guffaw and turned away from her, happy to see anything other than her face. An unwelcome image of her naked and wearing only red lipstick kept superimposing itself over the real Hazel. How long would it take before the disgusting dream faded from his mind?

A spring clean over the weekend might help. The first thing he needed to do would be to throw out *Guilty Pleasures* and *Guilty Pleasures: Love-cuffed liaisons.* Ariana was in the past. He needed to move on. He didn't know why his brain had chosen to mix up his new neighbour with his gorgeous ex. Hazel didn't resemble Ariana in any way. The only explanation was that Ariana dominated his thoughts so much, and Hazel was the person he had seen most often since arriving in the village, so his unconscious mind had fused them together in his nightmares.

Seemed as rational an explanation as any.

Jack arrived to his office building ten minutes early. Perfect. Just enough time to make a coffee before getting stuck into his files. Normally he didn't like caffeine, preferring Rooibos Tea, but his banging headache called for a sizeable dose of caffeine.

He went into the communal lounge and took off his coat, ready to hang it on the rack, but stopped in his tracks. Only one coat hung on the rack: a long, brown fur coat. He closed his eyes and shook his head, just in case it was another intrusive thought, then opened them.

Nope; the fur coat was still there.

That couldn't be Pamela's, could it? All week long, he had seen her wearing a long, grey puffer coat with a hood. Nothing as glamourous as a fur coat.

Jack hesitated before hanging his own coat on the rack. Unusual. Very unusual. What an unusual coincidence.

"Jack. How are you? Awfully cold today, isn't it?" Pamela's voice behind him caused him to jump.

"Oh, my goodness, sorry – I didn't mean to give you a fright."

She was wearing her usual long, grey puffer coat. M&S was more her style than S&M.

"That's okay – sorry I was so jumpy. Just lost in my thoughts." He gestured to the fur coat. “You wouldn’t know whose coat this is by any chance, would you?”

She gave an amused smile. “Doesn’t look like anything that would belong to Elaine on reception. Maybe it’s Colin’s. He left early yesterday and isn’t in today – maybe he got it for his wife and forgot to take it home.”

Good hypothesis, but Jack still felt needled by his thoughts. He was missing something; it didn’t add up. The coat looked similar to the one in his dream. In fact, *exactly* like the one in his dream. Odd coincidence. Very odd.

Work dragged by. He found he couldn’t concentrate on his paperwork, and definitely had lost his head for any Maths, as images from his dream kept popping into his mind and swamping his concentration. Hazel cavorting in nothing but red lipstick, her fur coat abandoned on the floor. He shut the blinds across the window in his office that looked across to the communal lounge; the fur coat hung at person-height and it reminded him of his nightmare.

Thank goodness it was Friday. He needed the weekend, with his friends and a few laughs, to reset. Too much had happened in a short few weeks: getting to know new neighbours; new-house issues and settling into a new job. He was overstimulated and welcomed some head-space.

His brow felt clammy with sweat. He dabbed it with a tissue and popped two ibuprofen tablets with a glass of water. Maybe he was coming down with a cold.

What would it matter if he knocked off a bit early? Fifteen minutes on a Friday afternoon wouldn’t matter too much, especially since the boss wasn’t even in the office.

Jack shut down his computer and put his paperwork away in the filing cabinet for Monday. He stuck his head into Pam’s office to say goodbye, then went into the communal lounge to grab his coat.

The fur coat was gone.

It seemed someone had maybe taken it while he had been working with the blinds shut in his office, and Pam had been busy with her own work. He dropped his gaze to the floor, where a small dusting of breadcrumbs lay scattered at the base of the coat stand.

Odd. He took the stairs down to reception. There were a few more crumbs scattered down the stairwell, as though someone had been eating a biscuit along the way as they left. Elaine was taking a call. He hung back beside reception until she finished then approached her with a smile.

"Elaine, I was just wondering if you know whether anyone came in today to pick up a coat?"

She frowned. "A coat?"

"A fur coat. You know, like a long, glamorous fur coat. The sort you'd wear in the evening to, say, a formal dinner."

She smirked, her eyes wide. "Sounds interesting. Must belong to a client of Pam's or Colin's."

"Pam doesn't know anything about it. It was hanging on the rack in the lounge when I got in this morning. I thought you might have seen someone about?"

She shook her head. As the phone rang with another call, Elaine mouthed silently for him to have a good weekend and gave him a wave. Jack waved back and mouthed the same back to her.

No lead on that, then. He put the coat out of his mind and enjoyed the walk home.

As his house came into view, he noticed a head of short brown hair bobbing along by the fence. Hazel was probably still gardening, as she had said earlier that day. It took him a moment to realise that she wasn't in her garden at all and was in fact inside his.

Hazel looked up as he approached his front gate. Her deer in headlights face quickly changed to her usual grin.

"Hello neighbour. You're home early, I see."

Jack's forehead tensed. "Oh yeah? How did you know what time I'd be home?"

A faint tinge of pink appeared on her cheeks. "Didn't you say earlier?"

He shook his head. "Not that I recall. Is there a problem?"

She gave a jovial laugh and waved her hand dismissively. "Nothing to worry about. I just thought I saw Izzy's cat, Buster, lurking near your shed. He's been missing for a few days after she had him wormed. He's normally a house cat, so I thought I would grab him for her, but by the time it took me to come over to your side, he was gone."

Convenient. Jack folded his arms across his chest. "Well, if I see him, I'll let Izzy know. She owns the bakery, doesn't she?"

Hazel's smile faltered. "Yes, but don't trouble yourself. You could let me know and I'll tell her instead."

He could have seen that excuse coming a mile away. Jack said nothing.

"I tell you what. How about I give you my number and you could tell me if he comes back?" she said, her tone an octave higher than usual; almost pleading.

"Why don't you give me Izzy's number instead and I'll shoot her a text directly if I see him in my garden?" he replied.

Hazel flapped her hand. "No need. I'm sure he won't come back. I'll give Izzy an update that he's on his way home."

For once, his neighbour was quick to excuse herself and brisk walked out of his garden and into her own, with only a quick wave goodbye over the fence. Jack watched her until her front door was shut, then went into his own house. There was no doubt in his mind; she had been lying about her reason for being in his garden.

What was Hazel up to? More to the point, why would she lie about it? He couldn't explain why he felt antsy; but he knew the only solution was to go and find out more information. He would start with Izzy.

It took a ten-minute walk to the main street. Quite a lucky decision in hindsight that he had chosen to leave work early, as that meant the shops were still open. The light was still on in the bakery, and the sign in the window read that it closed at five thirty, so that gave him about twelve minutes to have a word with her.

He saw her straight away in the storeroom behind the counter, checking the cash from the register. He waited until she had finished counting the money, so as not to distract her. A few minutes later, she looked up and caught sight of him. Her serious face broke into a wide, warm smile.

"It's Jack, isn't it? How lovely to see you again. You must have been tempted by the look of some of my cakes at the autumn fair and decided to try some," she teased.

He pressed his mouth into a tight-lipped smile. "Actually, I came here to ask after your cat, Buster. Hazel was saying she saw him in my garden earlier and that he'd run away after you got him wormed. I was just wondering if I could get your number to give you a call if he turns up again."

Izzy's smile dropped, leaving her expression glassy-eyed and vacant.

Was his suggestion too personal? "Or, your work number for this bakery, just so I could give you a ring."

She shook her head. "It isn't that. Buster is dead."

"Dead? I'm sorry to hear that. Did it happen today?"

"No, about a month ago. Hazel was minding him, while he recovered from the worming tablets. I didn't want to leave him alone while I was here all day, you see, and she's at home all the time. She's a painter, I'm sure you might know."

He thought of the disturbing paintings of men decorating her living room walls; that made sense. "Actually, I didn't know. I didn't know her job, or that Buster was dead. I'm so sorry."

"Don't be. It wasn't your fault, luvvie." She stretched her arm towards him, as though to console him from afar.

"What happened, if you don't mind me asking?"

"Hazel said he took a bad turn, as though he was coughing up a hairball, but he just choked and died."

Jack paused, composing his thoughts. "What do you think happened?"

"I don't know. Honestly it's a mystery. That was around the time Hazel hurt her foot." She suddenly broke into a nervous chuckle. "I said to Sam, my son, that maybe she tripped over Buster, got annoyed and poisoned him. But that would be ridiculous, wouldn't it?"

Jack swallowed. His throat felt dry all of a sudden.

He allowed his thoughts to meander back to the previous evening. His sudden sleepiness after dinner, and the strange nightmare. Could there have been a chance – however small – that he *hadn't* dreamed of

Hazel cavorting naked? What if she had drugged him by plying the jug or orange juice in his fridge with sleeping tablets?

The dryness in his throat was becoming an uncomfortable lump. He felt sick. Sick to the pit of his stomach.

"Sorry I stirred up painful memories of Buster. Thanks for your time," he said, and left the bakery.

What was going on? He thought back to the very first day he had met Hazel. Could Hazel have been *messing* with his head from the very start? Could his neighbour have been gaslighting him the whole time?

He roved over all the details. He was sure now that Hazel had made the macaroons and left them off to his workplace. Elaine was often away from her desk; it would be easy for someone to slip in unnoticed.

How about the handmade card with a picture of birds, so soon after he had been birdwatching while leaving the convenience store? Again, Hazel could have followed him at a distance while subtly spying on him. She was an artist by trade; a hand-painted card was an easy thing for her to make.

The baked goods and the card were easily explained, but other things were harder to account for. He was sure now that Hazel had seen the copy of *Guilty Pleasures* in the box by his front door, and had slipped the sequel through his letterbox, just to screw with him. But how could she have seen the photo of Ariana that he kept stored in his bedroom? Snooping while Stan was fixing his gas boiler, no doubt.

But what about the gas? Could that have been Hazel too?

How though? Prior to him lending her his key, how would she have got access to his house?

A lightbulb flashed on in his mind. *His open windows.* His complacency about a rural village being safer than London. Hazel could easily have reached, or climbed in, through his kitchen window while he had been out at work.

Jack shuddered.

He had literally been a victim of gaslighting – by having his own gas turned up to max. The problem was, he had no proof. Nothing. If he asked Hazel, she would deny it.

His mind was so preoccupied that he didn't realise he had walked to his workplace. His feet had taken him to the place where he *might* be able to get another question answered.

Elaine was grabbing her coat and bag. Looked like she was getting ready to leave. Pam was waiting for her in the reception area. Maybe they were planning to go for drinks after work. It was a Friday evening after all; the thought made him feel slightly bad as he was about to keep them running late.

"Jack? What brings you back? Did you forget something?" said Pam.

"Erm, no. Not exactly. I have a quick question, if that's alright. It's about that fur coat earlier. I'm just curious – there isn't CCTV in the office, is there?"

Both women's eyebrows shot upwards.

"Has something happened?" said Elaine.

How could he phrase his thoughts without sounding like a paranoid maniac? "I think I might know who the coat belongs to, and I wanted to see if I'm right. If I am, she'll show up on the CCTV, either this morning when she dropped it off, or later in the afternoon – possibly on your lunchbreak, Elaine – when she took it away."

Elaine's mouth dropped. "Well, it's such a quiet area around here that we've never needed it, but yes. We do have CCTV. We used it once to see what had damaged the glass front doors once during a storm, and got our insurance updated as a result. Stuff like that, you know."

"Would you mind if I had a quick look at the CCTV, just to see? Just for five minutes?"

"We can't access the CCTV unless we think there's a problem," she said.

"What if it was for something that turned out to be *potentially* linked to other things?" he said, careful to choose his words.

Elaine chewed her lower lip. "Not a crime, surely?"

"If I'm right, a woman is involved – and if I'm *doubly* right, I think she was in my house too," he elaborated.

Elaine and Pamela both looked shocked. "If it's a crime, you should report it to the police," said Elaine, holding her hands up in protest.

"It's not exactly a *crime*. I think a new neighbour of mine was mistakenly in here – just like she was mistakenly on my property – when she was trying to do something *friendly*. A *misunderstanding*, if you like."

He was sure he was giving her the biggest puppy-dog eyes. Jack didn't often like to be manipulative, but sometimes, the right words – and the right, persuasive facial expressions, were called for.

"Sure, alright then. Just for a minute. It's on the monitor."

She started up her computer while he walked around behind her reception desk. He watched the thumbnail images as she trawled back on the program to earlier that day.

Jack watched the replay from that morning as a slim figure of a woman, wearing a long, dark-coloured mackintosh entered reception. She held a bulky carrier bag in her right hand. The grainy image wasn't particularly clear, but he could make out curly dark hair that sat to her shoulders. The woman went up the stairs and the video cut out at the first bend. It was enough proof for him: Hazel had really worn black, curly hair extensions in a way that resembled Ariana. She really had brought the fur coat to his workplace and put it in the communal lounge upstairs. She had most likely collected the coat during Elaine's lunchtime and gone to have her fake tan and hair extensions removed.

Nausea welled in his stomach. He no longer had any appetite for pizza with his friends, who would be arriving up from London at any moment.

He thanked Elaine and said goodbye to both of them. Guilt nagged a bit on Elaine's behalf; he didn't want her to land in any trouble with the company if it turned out she was leaving her desk, and hence reception unattended, more than she should have been. On the other hand though, he had the evidence that he needed. He could confront Hazel about why she had been in his workplace to leave the fur-coat. It might even give him an angle to confront her about her sick and sordid naked display in his living room.

Jack arrived back at his house long after sun had set. He was thankful for the dark winter afternoons; he wasn't in the mood to glimpse his disturbed neighbour spying on him. Just what was the deal with Hazel anyway? If she had really done all the things he thought she had done, then what on earth could be going through her mind – other than serious mental illness?

The red Ford Fiat 500 in his driveway meant that Sophie and Aman were already waiting for him. He rapped on the driver's side window and his friends greeted him with grins. Seeing them was a breath of fresh air; the change he needed. Village life, because of one disturbed individual, was making everything feel very claustrophobic. The only thing he was sorry about was that he hadn't decided to travel down to London to see them instead. Oh well. At the very least, he could get a lot of things off his chest. What would they make of all that had happened at Hazel's hands, in a short few weeks? He waited for them both to get out of Aman's car.

"Hey J," said Sophie, swooping her arms around him and linking her fingers in a tight bear hug.

"Yo, yo," said Aman, giving him a fist bump.

"Am I *ever* glad to see you two," said Jack.

Sophie opened the boot of Aman's car and brought out a huge bag of corn chips, while Aman grabbed a crate of beer. "We grabbed supplies on the way," she said.

Jack grinned. Sod clean living; it was an *exceptional* weekend to say the least. It called for something more *medicinal* to relay the news he had to tell them. He led the way into his house, then sure they were away from any neighbourly snooping, on Hazel's part, locked the door.

"Nice upgrade from your studio flat in Ealing. I'm impressed, bro." Aman nodded his approval as he peered around.

"Well, how's country life treating you?" Sophie hugged the party-sized bag of corn chips like a pillow.

Jack blew out a puff of air. "Not boring."

Aman grinned. "Are you being sarcastic?"

"Sadly no. One of my neighbours is rather – shall we say – interesting."

Sophie bulged her eyes. "This sounds juicy. Spill the beans, then. Interesting in what way? Is she hot?"

Jack pulled a face. "Er... no! Creepy is more like it."

He led them into the living room. "She's about forty-two. Her clothes and hair style are, like, straight out of the seventies. I mean, she puts my grandmother to shame the way she dresses. But wait till you hear the half of it."

Aman passed around beers. Jack cracked open his and supped, then wiped the froth off his lip. Where to start?

He told his friends everything, watching their wide-eyed expressions as he told what he conjectured about the macaroons at work, the strange coincidence of the handmade bird-watching card, and saw Sophie's jaw drop as he mentioned the dirty book he found pushed through his letter-box soon after Hazel had seen *Guilty Pleasures.* Both of them looked horrified as he relayed his theory about the gas heating changes in his house, and how he had left his house key with Hazel to let the engineer in. When he confided his suspicions about how his neighbour might have drugged his orange juice with sleeping tablets before cavorting naked in his living room, and the sordid acts that followed, Sophie's hand flew to her mouth and Aman spluttered on his beer.

"Wait though, it doesn't stop there," Jack went on.

"What, there's more?" Sophie gasped. "It can't get worse, surely?"

Jack inhaled and continued, telling about the fur coat in his office, Hazel's excuse about Buster the cat when he caught her snooping in his garden, how he had talked to Izzy at the bakery and found out the cat was dead, and finally what he saw on CCTV in his workplace.

Sophie and Aman stared at him; Sophie with a crisp midway to her mouth, and Aman holding the can of beer suspended below his opened mouth.

"What do you guys think? I mean, am I crazy? Has less than a fortnight in the country addled my brains?" said Jack.

Aman gulped. "Your neighbour sounds deranged."

"Yeah, like a proper wacko," Sophie added.

"You need to get a copy of that CCTV," said Aman, wavering a finger at him.

"I think Elaine was reluctant, though. I mean, it might show she was slacking off, taking too many tea breaks in the back office instead of minding the reception desk."

They fell silent, thinking.

"You should confront the crazy bitch." Sophie swigged her beer and wiped her lip on the back of her hand. "Tell her that you have proof and see what she says."

"That's risky though," said Jack. "What if she actually goes full psycho on me?"

Aman laughed. "You could take her, I'm sure. Stab her until she doesn't get up, then don't turn your back on her, or she'll come back to life."

Jack rolled his eyes. "It's not a *horror* movie."

Sophie smirked. "Sounds pretty close, if you ask me."

"I have to live beside her, I just bought this house. My parents would kill me if I told them I wanted to sell – they put the deposit down for me."

His friends blinked, as they all resumed ideas.

Sophie put her index finger up, like a kid in school with a great idea for the teacher. "I've got it! Don't you ever watch crime shows? We can dust for prints."

She loaded a video on her phone and they all leaned close to watch. Sophie rummaged in her bag and pulled out a powdered compact case and a makeup brush. Jack and Aman followed as she strode into the kitchen.

"You said she might have been tampering with your gas, right? So if she touched it, there would be fingerprints, wouldn't there?" she said.

Jack nodded; he could see where this was going.

Sophie removed the lid of her compact. The loose powder inside looked like talcum powder, only a bronze colour. Sophie was a fan of bronzers, which she didn't blend too well on her jawline, in Jack's opinion. She flicked her wrist so that some powder streaked across the white gas boiler, falling in an arc down the front of the panel. She did the same motion again two times until a copious amount of powder coated the gas boiler.

"Better not waste all of it, or you'll look like a ghost in the morning," Aman joked.

Sophie elbowed him in the ribs and he laughed. Jack didn't laugh, however. He watched intently as she lifted the wide, soft-bristled makeup brush and dusted the excess powder off the gas boiler.

"Well, I'll be fucking damned," said Jack.

Two small fingerprints showed close to the dial on the front of the panel. It looked like a woman's pinky finger and ring finger, as though someone had pressed both on the panel while they had used the other fingers to turn the dial. Sophie held her fingers close to the two prints; Jack could see they were belonged to a person of larger size than his petite friend. He held his own hand in a position close to the prints. The person's fingers would have been smaller than his own.

"That is fucking insane." Aman pointed at the prints. "They're definitely not yours, mate, they're too small. And I'll bet they're not the gas engineer's either."

"If there ever *was* a gas engineer. I'm dealing with a pathological liar, after all," said Jack.

"I wonder why your fingerprints don't show on the thing, though?" said Sophie.

Jack hesitated. "I don't rest my whole hand on the panel, though. When I'm turning the dial, that's the only thing I touch."

Sophie's expression glimmered with excitement. "Do you have sticky tape? I've got an idea. I've seen this on crime shows."

"Detective Sophie on the case," Aman laughed.

Jack searched in the kitchen drawers and found sticky tape; always handy for sealing sandwich bags. He passed the roll to Sophie. She carefully snapped off a strip and pressed it over the fingerprints, then peeled it off the gas boiler panel, revealing a perfect capture of the prints.

Jack shook his head, impressed. "You are a fucking genius, I swear."

"Don't ever make fun of my orange jawline again, baby," she winked. "You've got the bitch with this one. All you have to do now is confront her about what she did, show her this, and watch her squirm."

***

What time was it? Jack raised his head up off the armchair, where he had been sleeping, splayed sideways with his legs over the armrest and head dangling off the cushion. The upside-down alignment made his drunken dizziness even more pronounced.

Sophie was asleep on her side, curled up on the sofa and Aman lay on the floor, with his hands crossed over his chest. Jack guffawed; his university friend slept like a vampire in a 1930s Hollywood movie. The entire living room floor, from sofa to TV, was littered with beer cans and empty vodka bottles. At some point, once they had chugged their way through the crate of beer, they had gone for a drunken walk to the off-licence on the other side of the village. Jack recalled little else of the evening.

What had woken him? The heat. The heat was unbearably high. This time he knew it was not a fluke. He hadn't thought to check the gas dial when they had returned from their trip to the off-licence. If he had, he was sure it would have been cranked up to the max.

His intuition made him turn again towards his sleeping friends. Sophie's bare legs glimmered with wet patches, as though water had dripped on them – or saliva. He looked again at Aman. There were wet splotches on his chin and neck. What about himself? Come to think of it, his toes felt tacky, as though they had been sucked and now were partially dry. He felt queasy.

A creak on the floorboards in the hallway roused him, and a subtle, barely audible swish; like a door brushing over a mat. He dashed out into the hall. His door keys were swinging in the keyhole. As he looked down, he saw the telltale signs of crumbs on the wooden floorboards. Proof! Hazel had been in his house.

Jack opened the door and ran barefoot into his garden. In the cold, wet, rainy early hours of whatever ungodly time-AM it was, he saw a dark silhouette dashing up the front steps and into her house, silent as a cougar on the prowl.

Fuck! If only he had thought to bring his phone; he would have had photographic proof of her crazymaking antics.

He went back into his house and locked the door, then stood looking at the key, his mind rampant with thoughts. When the three of them had left for the off-licence, had he locked the house? It wouldn't have mattered; he was positive now that Hazel had made a copy of his front door key when he had lent it to her to let the gas engineer in. On the way back, he was sure he had left the door unlocked; his keys in the keyhole would have blocked her spare key from turning, if it had been locked.

Gone were his days of carelessness; in the morning, he would call a locksmith and have all the doors and windows in his house refitted with new locks.

Jack went through his house, feeling every radiator. As suspected, they were warm, but not hot. Someone had tried to turn the heating up to gaslight him, and then turn it back down, so as not to get caught. Did Hazel not sleep?

"What's going on?"

Sophie's voice behind startled him, and he turned to see her rubbing her bleary eyes.

"You scared the shit out of me!"

She chortled. "Did you think I was your psycho neighbour?"

"Yes actually," he said, not returning the mirth.

Her face sobered. "Why, has something happened?"

He nodded. "She was in here. She got in while we were sleeping."

Sophie let her jaw drop. "You're shitting me? What was she doing – trying to rub out the finger prints?"

Before he could stop her, Sophie marched to the kitchen window and opened it wide. "Too late you crazy bitch – we already got proof of your perverted prints all over Jack's boiler. You leave my friend alone or we'll have you thrown in prison!"

Jack leaned against the door jamb, folding his arms across his chest. "Can the police really do that? Could we give them the prints and press charges, and they'd lock her away?"

Sophie gave a non-committal shrug. "Don't seriously know. Probably not. She hasn't stolen anything, so they couldn't get her on burglary."

"But it's proof of breaking and entering, is it not?" he countered.

She twitched her nose. "The psycho bitch would just say you invited her in. She made you that first batch of cookies after all, didn't she? She'd tell them you were friends."

A sudden surge of anger welled up like a volcano simmering in Jack. He couldn't let Hazel get away with what she had done. He turned on his heel and marched to the front door, Sophie chirping her excitement behind him as she followed. The commotion woke Aman, who followed too. Down the garden path, up Hazel's garden path. Three steps to her front door, then three loud raps on her door.

"Why, hello, Jack. Quite early for a visit," she said, in a cheerful purr.

Time to cut to the chase. "What were you doing in my house?"

She twitched one eyebrow upwards in a dramatic expression of faux-confusion. "I beg your pardon?"

"Don't play dumb. You were in my house a few minutes ago turning off the heating. What dangerous game are you playing at?"

Her grin showed feigned ignorance. "I'm afraid I don't know what you're talking about. I was asleep. You woke me just now. Perhaps you were dreaming. Were you dreaming of me Jack? How very neighbourly."

Jack had never wanted to punch someone so much in his life. He clenched his fists on either side of his hips but resisted the urge to let his anger bubble up.

"Just so you know, I have proof of what you've been doing. I have your fingerprints that were on my gas boiler. You were caught on CCTV at my workplace going in to get the fur coat that you left in the staff lounge. Ever heard of breaking and entering? I could have you locked up."

Hazel continued grinning, unabated. "I really don't know what you're talking about. Do you maybe have a temperature? It *is* flu season, after all."

He turned to either side, seeing Sophie and Aman flanking him on either side. Even though they didn't speak up for him, their presence gave him renewed courage. "I'm getting my locks changed today, Hazel, so don't think you can try any of your antics again. You're sick – and twisted. Stay away from me from now on, you got that?"

Hazel cocked her head to one side and puckered her mouth in mock sympathy. "I'm sorry you feel that way, Jack. I thought we were getting along just swimmingly."

Was she for real? Jack stared at her, unable to believe his ears.

Sophie gasped behind him. "Are you kidding, lady? We're friends of Jack's and he told us everything you did – including the stuff you did in his living room. There's places for sick fucks like you."

Hazel blinked at Sophie as though she was an annoying bug buzzing round her head; though his neighbour didn't drop her rehearsed smile.

"You must be Sophie. Any friend of Jack's is a friend of mine." A bland platitude in a pantomime voice.

Jack watched Sophie recoil as Hazel said her name. He studied Hazel's face, unwilling to comprehend what he was hearing. Was she deluded, or just a complete sociopath, with no understanding of what she had done wrong? She had no recognition of what she had done. No remorse. Certainly no repentance.

"Why don't you *all* come in for tea and cookies and we can talk through *all* of your troubles? Sophie and Aman are very welcome too," she said, her voice smooth as silk.

"How do you know our names?" Aman demanded.

Hazel gave a knowing smile. "Jack was kind enough to divulge them. And then I found out more about you – what I needed to know. *Sophie*, it must be so hard coming off antidepressants. Especially how your bosses would feel, since it *does* affect your job, after all. Why don't you talk it out over a cup of tea? And Aman. You should be *honest* with your fiancée about what you got up to at that stag do two weeks ago. I'm *sure* she would forgive you, especially since you two will be tying the knot next year."

Jack glared at her, waiting for his turn.

Hazel turned to him, unblinking. "As for you, wouldn't you want to know why Ariana broke up with you after Turkey? She's a lovely girl, that one. You shouldn't have let her slip through your fingers, silly boy."

Another surge of anger rose; Jack fought to control himself. "Have you been in touch with my ex? What is this – blackmail?"

Did the mask waver, for a split second? Did the corner of her mouth tremor? Did her cheek muscle twitch, revealing the face beneath the façade?

Maybe. But it was back in place, just as fast.

"I've made some gingerbread cookies. Wouldn't it be better to be amicable than disagreeable?"

Aman scowled, gave a curt nod, and crossed the threshold into Hazel's house.

"Come inside where it's warm and we can talk everything through."

Gingerbread cookies. A trail of breadcrumbs.

Sophie followed Aman inside, looking defeated. Jack's instincts screamed at him not to go with them. Against his better senses, he put his foot inside his neighbour's hallway and stepped in after his friends. Had Hazel been in touch with Ariana, or was it more lies?

Gingerbread cookies in a gingerbread house; a place for a witch, in the deep, dark countryside. A breadcrumb trail leading to a place of cookies. And lies.

Would he become another disturbing painting on her living room wall? Maybe. Or maybe not. Not if the witch ended up in her own oven to stew in her own juices, first.

Other books by Leilanie Stewart

Diabolical Dreamscapes: Strange and macabre short stories

Reader beware! From the hallucinatory imagination of Leilanie Stewart, author of award-winning ghost horror novel, The Blue Man, comes twenty-one previously published short stories and flash fiction, now entombed between the covers of a new darkly themed collection.

In Part 1: Dark and Surreal Tales of Death: Corpses find new purposes in death while fated to walk the earth and surreal journeys of the afterlife abound, involving trips to far-reaching corners of the earth, the moon, or Venus during the last throes of life.

In Part 2: Strange and Hallucinatory Stories of the Mind: Cats, rabbits, dogs, birds and spiders have a role to play in these dreamlike journeys through the mind, helping the characters of each tale unravel their fears and anxiety, while facing their darkness, depression and demons.

Available from Amazon, Waterstones, Barnes & Noble, Foyles and other retailers.

Matthew's Twin

Belfast Ghosts – Standalone Book 3 of 3: The spirit of medieval vengeance made flesh

A medieval Scottish soldier.
An Anglo-Irish witch.
A seven hundred year plot for revenge.

Around the time Customs Inspector Matthew began having crippling stomach pains, he began witnessing visions of a past-life involving a Scottish soldier during Edward Bruce's conquest of Ireland, an Anglo-Irish defender of Carrickfergus Castle and a local witch with a bloodthirsty agenda. When medieval mercenary and vengeful witch performed a necromantic ritual to help the Scottish conquest succeed, Matthew began to learn more about his connection with 14th century Northern Ireland.

After an operation to remove what he thought to be a tumour from his stomach, a mysterious man arrived to cause chaos in Matthew's life. What did the strange – yet familiar – man have to do with him? Why did malign forces from a dark, medieval past want to cause harm? Was there any way for Matthew to learn about a seven hundred year injustice before the ghosts came to wreak vengeance on him in the present?

Available from Amazon, Waterstones, Barnes & Noble, Foyles and other retailers.

The Fairy Lights

Belfast Ghosts – Standalone Book 2 of 3: The ghost of Christmas that never was

Author Shout Reader Ready Awards – Recommended Read 2024 winner

When Aisling moves into an old, Edwardian house in the university area of Stranmillis, Belfast, she soon discovers that her student digs are haunted. The house, bought by her grandfather decades ago, is also home to a spirit known by the nickname Jimbo.

As yuletide approaches, and Aisling's Christmas fairy lights attract mischief from Jimbo, she seeks to find out more about the restless entity. With the help of a local psychic and friends from her History with Irish course, Aisling uncovers dark, buried truths. What is the connection with Friar's Bush Graveyard just around the corner? What does Jimbo's dusty book of the Oak King and Holly King, hidden in the attic, have to reveal? What will Aisling's journey into the darkness of the spirit world reveal about Jimbo – and herself?

Available from Amazon, Waterstones, Barnes & Noble, Foyles and other retailers.

The Blue Man

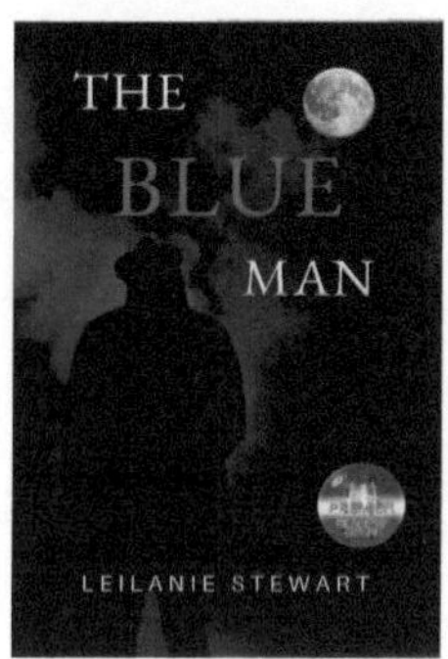

Belfast Ghosts – Standalone Book 1 of 3: A haunted friendship across the decades

Chill with a Book Premier Readers' Award and Book of the Month winner, February 2023

Two best friends. An urban legend. A sinister curse.

Twenty years ago, horror loving Sabrina told her best friend, Megan, the terrifying Irish folk tale of the Blue Man, who sold his soul to the Devil in vengeance against a personal injustice. What should have been the best summer of their schooldays turned into a waking nightmare, as the Blue Man came to haunt Megan. Sabrina, helpless to save Megan from a path of self-destruction and substance abuse as she sought refuge from the terror, left Belfast for a new life in Liverpool.

Twenty years later, the former friends reunited thinking they had escaped the horrors of the past. Both were pregnant for the first time. Both had lived elsewhere and moved back to their hometown, Belfast. Both were wrong about the sinister reality of the Blue Man, as the trauma of their school days caught up to them – and their families.

Why did the Blue Man terrorise Megan? Was there more to the man behind the urban legend? Was their friendship – and mental health – strong enough to overcome a twenty year curse?

Available from Amazon, Waterstones, Barnes & Noble, Foyles and other retailers.

The Buddha's Bone

She was in Japan to teach English. She'd soon discover the darker side of travelling alone.

Death

Kimberly Thatcher wasn't an English teacher. She wasn't a poet. She wasn't an adventurer. Now she wasn't even a fiancée. But when one of her fellow non-Japanese colleagues tried to make her a victim, she said no.

Cremation

In Japan on a one-year teaching contract at a private English language school, and with her troubled relationship far behind her in London, Kimberly set out to make new friends. She would soon discover the darker side of travelling alone – and people's true intentions.

Rebirth

As she came to question the nature of all those around her – and herself – Kimberly was forced to embark on a soul-searching journey into emptiness. What came next after you looked into the abyss? Could Kimberly overcome the trauma – of sexual assault and pregnancy loss –

blocking her path to personal enlightenment along the way, and forge a new identity in a journey of–

Death. Cremation. Rebirth.

Available from Amazon, Waterstones, Barnes & Noble, Foyles and other retailers.

Gods of Avalon Road

London, present day.

Kerry Teare and her university friend Gavin move to London to work for the enigmatic Oliver Doncaster. Their devious new employer lures them into an arcane occult ritual involving a Golden Horse idol.

Britannia, AD 47.

Aithne is the Barbarian Queen of the Tameses tribes. The Golden Warrior King she loves is known as Belenus. But are the mutterings of the Druids true: is he really the Celtic Sun God himself?

Worlds collide as Oliver's pagan ritual on Mayday summons gods from the Celtic Otherworld of Avalon. Kerry is forced to confront the supernatural deities and corrupt mortals trying to control her life and threatening her very existence.

Leilanie Stewart is an award-winning author and poet from Belfast, Northern Ireland. She writes paranormal and psychological fiction, as well as experimental verse. Her writing confronts the nature of self; her novels feature main characters on a dark psychological journey who have a crisis and create a new sense of identity. She began writing for publication while working as an English teacher in Japan, a career pathway that has influenced themes in her writing. Her former career as an Archaeologist has also inspired her writing and she has incorporated elements of archaeology and mythology into both her fiction and poetry.

In addition to promoting her own work, Leilanie runs Bindweed Anthologies, a creative writing publication with her writer husband, Joseph Robert. Aside from publishing pursuits, Leilanie enjoys spending time with her husband and their lively literary lad, a voracious reader of sea monster books.

www.leilaniestewart.com

Acknowledgements

Acknowledgements are due to Roxana Nastase for first publishing Leah as the Artist's Muse in Scarlet Leaf Review in 2017. Cover and internal image elements with thanks to Canva.

Thank you to my hubby and editor, Joseph Robert, for the story feedback and polish and also your feedback on the graphic design of the cover.

I've also met some awesome fellow authors through the Instagram community –

Rosalind Barden: (www.rosalindbarden.com)

Amanda Sheridan
(www.instagram.com/amandasheridanauthor)
(www.facebook.com/profile.php?id=100063878022530)

Laura Lyndhurst: (https://www.facebook.com/lauralyndhurstauthor/)

Please do check out their fabulous writing and follow them on social media.

Last, but not least, thanks to you for buying my book. Having readers keeps me motivated to write more stories, so just to let you know that I appreciate you taking the time to read and review my books. It means more than you know.

www.ingramcontent.com/pod-product-compliance
Lightning Source LLC
Chambersburg PA
CBHW030544310726
48979CB00010B/2020/J

* 9 7 8 1 7 3 9 4 8 1 9 3 3 *